CW01082919

Witchy Wonders: Halloween at the Zoo

Ella Dia

Published by Bright Minds Books, 2024.

WITCHY WONDERS: HALLOWEEN AT THE ZOO

First edition. October 22, 2024.

Copyright © 2024 Ella Dia.

ISBN: 979-8224077502

Written by Ella Dia.

Table of Contents

Chapter 1: A Mysterious Invitation...1

Chapter 2: The Enchanted Entrance...5

Chapter 3: The Disappearing Bats 9

Chapter 4: The Ghostly Giraffes 14

Chapter 5: Don's Discovery of the Phantom Wolves 18

Chapter 6: Timmy's Encounter with the Trickster Monkeys........23

Chapter 7: Jake's Escape from the Gargoyle Garden....................29

Chapter 8: The Pumpkin Patch Puzzle 34

Chapter 9: Don's Trial of Wit..38

Chapter 10: The Haunted Aquarium...42

Chapter 11: The Enchanted Carousel..46

Chapter 12: The Midnight Menagerie..50

Chapter 13: The Final Showdown with Mr. Grimble 57

Chapter 14: The Celebration of Lights..61

Chapter 15: The Shadowy Zookeeper 65

Chapter 16: New Beginnings...69

Chapter 17: Guardians of the Sanctuary......................................73

Chapter 18: The Return of Shadows..77

Chapter 19: Uncharted Waters 82

Chapter 20: A Call to Adventure...87

Chapter 21: The Depths of the Sanctuary 92

Chapter 22: The Whispering Woods 97

Chapter 23: The Trial of Echoes.. 102

Chapter 24: The Heart of the Woods 106

Chapter 25: Secrets of the Woods.. 111

Description

In *Witchy Wonders: Halloween at the Zoo*, young guardians Don, Mandy, Timmy, and Jake embark on a magical adventure through a vibrant zoo filled with enchanting creatures and hidden wonders.

As they discover their unique powers and face challenges, they must protect the sanctuary from lurking shadows. With each trial, they learn the importance of friendship, courage, and the magic that connects them all.

Join these brave friends as they navigate the Whispering Woods, unlock ancient secrets, and prove that together, they can overcome even the darkest fears. This whimsical tale celebrates the power of unity and the magic of Halloween.

Dedication

For the dreamers and adventurers, may you always believe in the magic around you. To the friends who stand by you through every challenge, let your bonds be your greatest strength. And for every child who dares to embrace their imagination—may your journeys be filled with wonder and joy.

Preface

Witchy Wonders: Halloween at the Zoo invites readers into a world where friendship and magic intertwine.

This story emerged from the desire to explore themes of bravery, unity, and the importance of believing in oneself. As our young guardians traverse enchanting landscapes and face their fears, they discover that true strength lies in their bonds. Set against the backdrop of Halloween, this tale emphasizes the power of imagination, the joy of adventure, and the magic that exists all around us. It is a celebration of courage, curiosity, and the indomitable spirit of friendship.

Join Don, Mandy, Timmy, and Jake on their unforgettable journey, and let the magic inspire you to embrace your own adventures!

Chapter 1: A Mysterious Invitation

Don was sprawled out on the living room floor, flipping through the channels on the TV, when a soft tapping echoed from the window. He paused, sat up, and blinked at the glass, half-expecting to see a bird. Instead, a small, yellowed envelope was stuck to the pane, its edges glowing faintly in the dim light of the room.

"Hey, Mandy!" he called, not taking his eyes off the window. "Come look at this!"

His sister, Mandy, rushed in from the kitchen, wiping her hands on her jeans. "What is it this time, Don?" she asked, clearly expecting one of his usual pranks.

Without answering, Don pointed to the window. Mandy followed his gaze and gasped. "Where did that come from?"

"I don't know. It just appeared."

They exchanged a glance before Don raced outside, Mandy right behind him. The air had a sharp chill, a typical autumn evening on the eve of Halloween. Don carefully peeled the envelope from the window and turned it over in his hands. No address. No stamp. Only a seal—a wax seal with the imprint of a witch's hat.

Curiosity boiling over, he tore it open. Inside was a thick piece of parchment with swirling letters written in deep purple ink:

"You are cordially invited to the most mysterious, magical, and spooky event of the year: Halloween at the Zoo. Join us for a night of surprises, creatures beyond imagination, and adventures unlike any you've experienced before. The gates open at 7 PM sharp. Follow the moon, and you'll find your way."

There was no signature, no further explanation, just a sense of intrigue hanging in the air.

"Are you serious?" Mandy whispered. "This sounds awesome!"

Before Don could respond, their front door burst open and Timmy, Don's best friend, came running up, waving an identical letter in his hand. "Did you guys get one of these?" he asked, out of breath.

"We did," Don said, showing him the invitation.

"You too?" a familiar voice chimed in. It was Jake, Mandy's friend, notorious for pulling pranks and causing mischief. He was standing at the end of the driveway, clutching his own letter, a mischievous gleam already dancing in his eyes.

"This has to be a joke, right?" Timmy asked, though he didn't sound convinced.

"No way. This is legit," Mandy said. "Look at the seal, the parchment—it feels... different."

The four of them stood in silence for a moment, considering the strange turn of events.

Don finally broke the quiet. "So, are we going or not?"

Mandy's eyes lit up, and Timmy hesitated but gave a small shrug. Jake, always ready for an adventure, grinned wide. "We're going. This sounds too good to pass up."

That night, the excitement was palpable as the four friends prepared for the unknown. Costumes packed, flashlights at the ready, and a lingering sense of mystery wrapped around their thoughts. The zoo was always interesting during the day, but this Halloween night promised something far more extraordinary.

The next evening, just as the sky turned a deep shade of orange, Don, Mandy, Timmy, and Jake set off. They followed the directions given in the letter, taking a narrow path that led through the woods toward the outskirts of town. The moon, unusually full and bright, guided their way, casting long shadows across the trees.

As they approached the zoo, an eerie calm settled over the air. The usual sounds of traffic and the rustling of leaves seemed distant, muted by the thick fog that began to swirl around their feet. The towering iron gates of the zoo loomed ahead, covered in vines and glowing softly under the moonlight. Twinkling lanterns lined the path leading up to the entrance, illuminating strange shapes carved into the surrounding trees—witches, pumpkins, and other spooky symbols.

"Well, this is... different," Timmy muttered, his eyes wide as they stepped closer to the gate.

Just then, a deep, smooth voice broke the silence.

"Welcome, welcome, young adventurers." A figure appeared from behind the gate, draped in a long, flowing robe the color of midnight. Her hair, streaked with silver, tumbled down in waves. Her pointed hat was perched atop her head, and her eyes shimmered with an unnatural glow.

"Who... who are you?" Jake stammered, trying to maintain his usual cool demeanor.

The woman gave a sly smile, her eyes locking on each of them in turn. "I am Zara, keeper of this zoo. Tonight, it is my duty to ensure you have a Halloween unlike any other. But, heed my warning—this zoo is not what you are used to. You may see things that defy explanation, creatures that belong to a world beyond your understanding. Stay on the path, and you'll be fine. But wander too far..." Her voice trailed off, leaving the warning hanging ominously in the air.

Don swallowed hard, feeling a thrill of excitement and a tinge of nervousness.

"Now, step inside. Your adventure awaits."

Zara waved her hand, and the iron gates creaked open. Beyond them lay the familiar zoo, but something was different. The trees seemed taller, the air felt thicker, and the exhibits—what little they could see—looked nothing like the daytime zoo they had visited before.

The four friends exchanged glances, then stepped through the gates.

Immediately, the air changed. The soft hum of nocturnal animals, which they were used to hearing in the distance, was replaced with low growls, eerie howls, and otherworldly whispers. The usual zoo signs pointing to various exhibits were now crooked, their writing altered—each one marked with strange symbols and riddles.

"Okay, this is definitely not your average zoo trip," Mandy whispered, her eyes darting around.

Jake, undeterred, moved ahead, eager to explore. "Come on, let's check it out."

They followed the winding path, the lanterns casting flickering shadows that danced across the ground. Suddenly, out of the mist, a shape appeared—tall and looming, with massive wings outstretched.

Timmy froze. "What is that?"

As the mist cleared, they realized it was an enormous statue of a bat, its wings spread wide in a protective stance. At its base was an inscription that none of them could read, written in a language that looked ancient and foreign. Beneath it, a small pedestal held four glowing stones, each with a different symbol etched into it.

Zara's voice echoed from somewhere nearby, though they couldn't see her. "To continue, each of you must choose a stone. Choose wisely, for the symbol you select will guide your path tonight."

Don, Mandy, Timmy, and Jake exchanged uncertain looks before stepping forward. Each one reached out to touch a stone, feeling a strange warmth radiate through their fingers.

One by one, they picked up the stones, the symbols glowing brighter as they did.

Then, without warning, the ground beneath them began to tremble.

Chapter 2: The Enchanted Entrance

The ground beneath them vibrated like the purring of a large animal, soft yet undeniably powerful. Don's heart raced as he glanced at the glowing stone in his hand, the symbol on it shifting and pulsing with a warm, amber light. Beside him, Mandy clutched her own stone, her eyes wide but gleaming with excitement. Timmy, as cautious as ever, looked at his stone with a mix of awe and worry, while Jake seemed to relish the thrill of the unknown, his grin widening.

Suddenly, the rumbling stopped, leaving only an eerie silence in its wake. For a moment, the four stood frozen, unsure of what would happen next.

"What... what did we just do?" Timmy asked, his voice barely above a whisper.

Before anyone could answer, a soft rustling filled the air, like leaves swept by a breeze, but the night remained still. The sound grew louder, until it was impossible to ignore. Slowly, they turned their heads toward the source—the towering bat statue behind them. Its massive stone wings, which had been folded tight against its body moments ago, were now unfurling. Dust and debris fell from the ancient stone as the wings stretched wide, casting long shadows that danced across the zoo's foggy path.

Mandy gasped. "It's moving!"

With a soft grinding sound, the bat's head tilted, and its hollow eyes glowed a faint red. The pedestal at its base trembled, and the inscriptions, once unreadable, now flickered with light. The glowing stones in their hands seemed to react, humming gently in response.

"Welcome, travelers," a deep, echoing voice resonated from the statue. The voice, though commanding, carried a strange warmth. "You have been chosen to guide this night's events. Your paths are now bound to the creatures that reside in this zoo."

Don swallowed hard, his gaze fixed on the animated statue. "What does that mean?"

The bat's eyes brightened as it spoke. "You each hold a symbol of power. These symbols represent the different creatures of the zoo. Your task is to find your creature, for they will be your guide. But beware... not all creatures are as they seem."

Timmy's fingers tightened around his stone, a soft glow emanating from the carved crescent moon on its surface. "But how will we know which creature is ours?"

"Trust your instincts," the bat said, its wings folding back against its sides. "The symbols will reveal themselves in time. Follow the path, and you will discover more than you ever imagined. However, be cautious of the shadows—they are not what they appear."

Jake's grin stretched wider. "This is going to be fun."

Before anyone could respond, the bat statue's eyes dimmed, and the glow from the pedestal faded. The mist around them thickened, swirling into strange shapes that twisted and turned like ghostly figures.

"Looks like we're supposed to keep going," Mandy said, her voice steady despite the unnerving events.

Don nodded, still feeling the warmth of the stone in his hand. "Let's stick together. If the stones are supposed to guide us, we'll figure it out along the way."

With cautious steps, the group moved deeper into the zoo. The once-familiar paths were now transformed, winding in unexpected directions and lined with lanterns that flickered with ghostly green flames. The air felt heavy, as though it carried ancient secrets waiting to be uncovered.

As they walked, the sounds of the animals around them began to change. The familiar hoots of owls and the soft chirping of crickets were replaced with deep growls, eerie howls, and distant screeches. It was as if the creatures of the night were watching, waiting for the right moment to reveal themselves.

Timmy, ever the cautious one, stuck close to Don. "Do you think we'll actually meet these... creatures?"

"I don't know," Don admitted. "But I have a feeling that whatever we're supposed to find, it's not going to be normal."

Jake, walking ahead, suddenly stopped. "Check this out."

The group hurried to catch up with him, and they found themselves standing in front of a towering iron gate. The gate, much like the entrance to the zoo, was intricately carved with designs of strange animals—bats, wolves, and creatures they didn't recognize. Beyond the gate, the fog was thicker, swirling like a living thing.

But what really caught their attention was the plaque mounted on the gate. It was engraved with the same symbols that glowed on their stones.

"This must be it," Mandy said, her voice full of wonder.

Jake reached for the gate, but as soon as his fingers touched the cold iron, the ground shook again, this time more violently. The gate rattled, and the fog beyond it parted, revealing a long, winding path leading into a dense forest.

"The creatures are waiting," Zara's voice echoed from somewhere unseen. "Each of you must find the one that calls to you. But remember—the wrong choice will lead to peril."

Don looked at his stone again, the glowing symbol pulsating as if alive. "I think we're supposed to split up."

Timmy's face paled. "Split up? That sounds like a terrible idea."

But Jake, ever the daredevil, was already pushing the gate open. "Come on, Timmy. Where's your sense of adventure? We'll be fine. We've got these stones, right?"

Don hesitated, but Mandy stepped forward, her determination evident. "Jake's right. The stones are supposed to help us. Besides, we've come this far. We can't back out now."

Reluctantly, Timmy nodded. The four of them passed through the gate, stepping onto the path that would lead them into the unknown.

The moment they crossed the threshold, the gate creaked shut behind them, sealing them in.

The path ahead split into four directions, each one marked with a faint glow that matched the symbols on their stones.

Don studied the paths carefully. "Looks like each of us has to go a different way."

Mandy took a deep breath and squared her shoulders. "Guess this is it."

With that, they each chose their path, the stones in their hands guiding them forward. Don felt a tug in his chest as he stepped onto his path, his mind racing with questions. What creature was waiting for him? And would it truly be a guide—or something far more dangerous?

As he ventured deeper into the fog, the sounds of his friends faded into the distance. The world around him seemed to shift, the trees growing taller and the shadows lengthening with each step. The air felt colder, thicker, as if the very atmosphere was alive with magic.

Ahead, a pair of glowing eyes appeared in the darkness.

Don's heart skipped a beat, but he pressed on, clutching the stone tightly. The creature was waiting for him.

He just hoped he was ready.

Chapter 3: The Disappearing Bats

Don's pulse quickened as he moved along the path, the fog swirling around his feet. His stone continued to glow faintly, illuminating the trail ahead, but his thoughts were scattered. He couldn't shake the feeling that he was being watched. The trees loomed higher, their gnarled branches twisting like skeletal hands reaching for the sky. Every now and then, he thought he saw shadows darting between the trunks, but each time he turned to look, they were gone.

As he ventured deeper into the zoo's nocturnal maze, the sounds of his friends had long since faded. He clutched the glowing stone tighter, hoping it would lead him safely to whatever creature awaited him.

Suddenly, the path opened up into a wide clearing. Above, the canopy of trees thinned, revealing the full moon, large and gleaming against the dark sky. In the center of the clearing stood a grand stone structure—a massive, circular enclosure, its walls high and shrouded in ivy. Banners fluttered from tall poles, each one adorned with the same bat-like symbol that pulsed on his stone.

Don hesitated, taking in the strange sight before him. There was something almost sacred about the place, as if it had been there for centuries, waiting for this exact moment. He stepped forward, his sneakers crunching on the gravel beneath him, and approached the entrance. A pair of heavy wooden doors stood ajar, creaking softly as the wind pushed them to and fro.

He swallowed his nervousness and slipped inside.

The interior was dimly lit by lanterns that hung from the walls, casting flickering shadows across the vast space. Tall pillars lined the edges of the enclosure, and above them, bats circled in graceful arcs, their wings nearly silent as they cut through the air. They moved like shadows themselves, quick and elusive, only visible in brief glimpses as they swooped low or passed in front of the lanterns.

Don marveled at the creatures. He'd always liked bats—the way they seemed so mysterious, creatures of the night that most people misunderstood. But these bats were different. There was something almost... otherworldly about them, the way they seemed to blend into the darkness so perfectly.

As Don watched, one of the bats broke away from the group and swooped down toward him. He tensed, unsure of what to expect, but the creature simply hovered in front of him, its wings flapping gently. Its eyes gleamed in the dim light, intelligent and knowing.

The bat didn't speak, but Don felt a strange connection with it, almost as if it were communicating without words. It was a guide, he realized, just like the statue had said. But what was it guiding him to?

Without warning, the bat soared upward, rejoining the others as they circled above. Don stared after it, trying to make sense of the encounter. But then, something even stranger happened.

One by one, the bats began to disappear.

At first, Don thought it was a trick of the light. The bats would swoop behind a pillar or vanish into the shadows, only to reappear a moment later. But as he watched, it became clear that they weren't coming back. They were vanishing completely—gone as if they had never been there at all.

Panic surged through him. What was happening? He scanned the enclosure, searching for any sign of the bats, but the air above was empty. The lanterns flickered wildly, casting erratic shadows across the stone walls, and an eerie silence fell over the space.

Then, out of the darkness, a voice called his name.

"Don..."

He froze, his heart thudding in his chest. The voice was soft, almost like a whisper carried on the wind, but there was no mistaking it. Someone—or something—was calling for him.

"Don..."

The voice came again, closer this time. He spun around, trying to pinpoint its source, but the shadows seemed to shift and twist, making it impossible to focus.

"Who's there?" he called, his voice trembling slightly despite his efforts to stay calm.

There was no answer. Only silence, thick and oppressive.

Don's mind raced. The bats—why had they disappeared? And what was this voice? Was it part of the zoo's magic, or something else entirely? He had to find out.

Clutching his glowing stone, he took a deep breath and moved further into the enclosure. The pillars loomed on either side of him, their shadows long and dark. The voice didn't call again, but he could feel a presence—a sense that he wasn't alone.

The deeper he ventured, the more the atmosphere seemed to change. The air grew colder, the fog thickening until it was almost like a solid wall around him. The lanterns flickered erratically, their light dimming as if they, too, were being swallowed by the darkness.

Just as he was about to turn back, something caught his eye. At the far end of the enclosure, nestled between two pillars, was a small pedestal. Resting atop it was an ornate, black-and-silver box, its surface etched with strange, swirling symbols.

Don approached the pedestal cautiously. The box didn't look dangerous, but in a place like this, he couldn't be sure. The symbols on the box glowed faintly, their light pulsing in time with the glowing stone in his hand.

His fingers itched to open the box, but he hesitated. What if it was a trap? What if this was what had caused the bats to disappear?

But then he remembered Zara's words: *The symbols will guide you.* The stone had led him here for a reason. He had to trust it.

With a deep breath, Don reached out and placed his hand on the box. The moment his fingers touched the cool surface, the symbols flared to life, glowing brighter than before. The air around him seemed to hum with energy, and the box clicked open.

Inside, resting on a velvet cushion, was a small, intricately carved medallion. It was shaped like a bat in mid-flight, its wings outstretched, and its eyes glowed the same deep red as the statue's had earlier.

Don picked up the medallion, feeling a strange warmth spread through him. As he held it, the fog around him began to recede, and the enclosure seemed to come alive once more. The bats reappeared, swooping down from the shadows above, their graceful forms illuminated by the now-steady lanterns.

But there was something else. A presence.

From the far side of the enclosure, a figure emerged—a tall, slender man with pale skin and dark, piercing eyes. He was dressed in a long black coat, his hair slicked back, and his lips curved into a faint smile.

"Congratulations," the man said, his voice smooth and melodious. "You've found the Medallion of the Bat. Few have been able to locate it, and even fewer have earned its trust."

Don took a step back, clutching the medallion tightly. "Who are you?"

The man's smile widened. "My name is Barnaby. I am the keeper of the bats—and now, it seems, you are their chosen guide."

Don's mind spun. Chosen guide? What did that even mean?

Barnaby seemed to sense his confusion. "All in due time, my young friend," he said. "For now, take the medallion. It will protect you on the journey ahead. But remember—this is only the beginning. The true challenge lies beyond."

Without another word, Barnaby turned and disappeared into the shadows, leaving Don standing alone in the now-empty enclosure. The bats circled overhead, their wings brushing the air like whispers.

Don glanced down at the medallion in his hand, the weight of its importance settling over him. Whatever lay ahead, he knew he would need it.

Taking one last look at the bats, Don stepped back onto the path, ready to face whatever came next.

Chapter 4: The Ghostly Giraffes

Mandy's path led her through a dense thicket of trees, their branches arcing overhead to form a dark tunnel. The mist that swirled at her feet grew thicker the farther she ventured, making it difficult to see more than a few steps ahead. She clutched the glowing stone tightly in her hand, the soft light illuminating the path in front of her. A symbol shimmered on its surface—a crescent moon intertwined with delicate vines. It pulsed faintly, as if urging her forward.

Unlike Don's adventurous spirit, Mandy felt a sense of quiet resolve. She wasn't afraid, but the mystery surrounding the zoo's transformation had her on edge. The magic was everywhere—woven into the air itself—and the deeper she ventured, the more aware she became of its power. The trees seemed to whisper as she passed, their branches creaking and shifting as though alive.

Suddenly, the trees parted, and Mandy stepped into a wide, open clearing. In the center stood a large wooden fence surrounding a tall structure—a giraffe enclosure, but one unlike any she had seen before. The fenceposts were adorned with glowing runes, and strange shadows danced along the ground, flickering like the light from a distant fire.

She moved closer, her curiosity piqued. The wooden gate to the enclosure stood open, and a low hum seemed to emanate from inside. As she peered through the gate, she noticed something unusual about the enclosure. The grass shimmered with a pale, bluish glow, and the trees within seemed to move even though there was no wind. In the distance, she could make out the long, slender necks of several giraffes, their heads swaying gently as they wandered through the enclosure.

But these giraffes were different. Their bodies appeared translucent, their outlines flickering like images projected on a screen. The moonlight shone through them, casting faint, eerie shadows on the ground. They moved with an almost ghostly grace, their hooves making no sound as they glided through the glowing grass.

Mandy's heart skipped a beat. *Ghostly giraffes?* She had heard stories of haunted creatures before, but she had never imagined seeing anything like this.

She hesitated at the entrance, unsure whether to step inside. The giraffes didn't seem dangerous—just strange and ethereal—but the whole atmosphere felt otherworldly. She glanced down at the stone in her hand, its light pulsing in time with her heartbeat. The stone hadn't steered her wrong yet, and something about the enclosure called to her, as if it were waiting for her to explore it.

Taking a deep breath, Mandy stepped through the gate.

The moment her foot touched the glowing grass, a soft chime echoed through the air. The giraffes turned their heads in unison, their enormous eyes glowing softly in the darkness. They regarded her with a quiet intensity, their bodies shifting like ripples in water. For a moment, Mandy stood frozen, unsure of how to approach the strange creatures.

Then, one of the giraffes stepped forward, its long legs moving with a fluid, almost unnatural grace. As it drew closer, Mandy realized just how enormous it was—taller than any giraffe she had ever seen. Its translucent skin shimmered with a pale, silvery light, and its eyes, though kind, seemed to hold centuries of knowledge.

The giraffe lowered its head until its face was level with Mandy's. She stared into its glowing eyes, and for a moment, she felt as though the giraffe was looking straight into her soul.

A voice, soft and melodic, echoed in her mind. *"You've come for a reason, young one. The stars have guided you here."*

Mandy's eyes widened in shock. The giraffe was speaking—not aloud, but directly into her thoughts.

"I... I didn't know giraffes could talk," she stammered, unsure how to respond.

"Not all can," the giraffe replied, its voice soothing. *"But we are no ordinary giraffes. We are the guardians of the night, the keepers of forgotten dreams. This zoo holds many secrets, and we are but one of them."*

Mandy's mind raced. Guardians of the night? Forgotten dreams? This was unlike anything she had ever encountered before.

"What do you mean by forgotten dreams?" she asked, her voice barely a whisper.

The giraffe lifted its head slightly, its eyes still locked on hers. *"Long ago, this zoo was more than just a home for animals. It was a place where dreams took shape, where magic flowed freely. But over time, the world changed. People stopped believing in the old magic, and the creatures of the zoo began to fade. We are the remnants of that magic, the dreams that were lost."*

Mandy listened in awe, trying to absorb the giraffe's words. There was something both beautiful and sad about the idea of forgotten dreams—of magic slipping away as the world moved on.

"So... what can I do?" she asked, feeling a strange sense of responsibility. "How can I help?"

The giraffe regarded her for a long moment before answering. *"The magic still lives, but it is fragile. There are forces at work in this zoo, forces that seek to reclaim what was lost. But not all of those forces are kind. There are those who would twist the magic for their own purposes. Your task is to protect the light that remains, to guard it from those who would corrupt it."*

Mandy felt a chill run down her spine. She had known from the beginning that this night was different—that the zoo held secrets far beyond what she had imagined. But now, standing in front of the ghostly giraffe, she realized just how important her role was.

"What do I need to do?" she asked, her voice steady.

The giraffe tilted its head slightly, as if considering her question. *"You must find the source of the corruption. There is a darkness spreading through the zoo, a shadow that threatens to consume everything. You are not alone—there are others who will help you. But you must be vigilant. The path ahead will not be easy."*

Mandy nodded, determination filling her chest. "I'll do whatever it takes," she said firmly.

The giraffe's eyes softened, and it lowered its head once more. *"Take this,"* it said, gesturing with its long neck to a small object nestled in the grass. Mandy crouched down and picked it up, feeling a cool, smooth surface beneath her fingers. It was a small, crescent-shaped pendant, glowing with the same silvery light as the giraffe.

"This will protect you," the giraffe said. *"It holds the light of the stars, a reminder that even in the darkest night, there is always hope. Keep it close, and it will guide you when the shadows grow too strong."*

Mandy slipped the pendant into her pocket, feeling its reassuring weight against her skin. "Thank you," she said, her voice filled with gratitude.

The giraffe nodded, then stepped back, its long legs moving gracefully through the glowing grass. The other giraffes watched silently, their bodies flickering like fading lanterns in the distance.

Mandy stood for a moment, watching the ghostly creatures as they slowly disappeared into the mist. The air around her felt lighter, as though the weight of the world had been lifted from her shoulders. But she knew that the real challenge was still ahead. The giraffe's words echoed in her mind—*the darkness is spreading.*

She turned and made her way back to the entrance of the enclosure, her hand resting on the crescent pendant in her pocket. The path ahead was uncertain, but she felt a new sense of purpose burning inside her. She wasn't just exploring a magical zoo—she was part of something much bigger, something that could change everything.

Chapter 5: Don's Discovery of the Phantom Wolves

The cool air wrapped around Don like a thin mist as he stepped onto the winding path, feeling the weight of the medallion hanging from his neck. The faint glow of the stone in his hand pulsed softly, guiding him deeper into the enchanted zoo. Though he had felt a surge of confidence after discovering the Medallion of the Bat, a flicker of doubt nagged at him. What exactly had he gotten himself into?

The shadows thickened as he moved further away from the illuminated clearing, and the soft sounds of the night—rustling leaves, distant owls—began to fade. The path twisted like a snake, pulling him into the depths of the unknown. His heart raced with each step, the anticipation building like the suspense in a movie right before a thrilling reveal.

As he rounded a bend, the path opened into a secluded glen surrounded by towering trees whose branches reached skyward like skeletal fingers. At the far end of the glen stood a dense thicket, the entrance obscured by low-hanging branches and twisting vines. A deep growl resonated from within the shadows, sending a shiver down his spine.

"What was that?" Don muttered to himself, glancing around for any sign of movement. The air felt charged, thick with energy, as if the very forest was alive and watching him.

Then, he heard it again—a low, haunting growl, punctuated by the rustling of leaves. It was a sound that resonated deep within him, stirring both fear and excitement. Steeling his nerves, Don approached the thicket, pushing aside the branches that blocked his way.

As he stepped into the darkness, the growling intensified, echoing around him like a warning. Suddenly, a figure emerged from the shadows—a massive wolf, its fur as dark as the night itself. The wolf's eyes glowed with an otherworldly light, shimmering like stars in the sky. It stood tall and proud, exuding a sense of power that sent a thrill through Don.

"Who dares to enter my domain?" the wolf growled, its voice deep and resonant.

Don froze, caught off guard. "I—uh—I'm Don. I'm here for a reason."

The wolf narrowed its eyes, studying him with an intensity that made Don's heart race. "And what reason would that be?"

"I'm not sure yet," he admitted, feeling a mix of vulnerability and determination. "But I'm on an adventure. I want to help."

The wolf's expression shifted, a flicker of interest breaking through its fierce demeanor. "Help? You? What do you know of the magic in this place?"

"I've seen things—strange creatures, magical events. I found a medallion that connects me to the bats. I think I'm supposed to protect something."

The wolf stepped closer, the ground beneath its paws silent as it approached. "You speak of protection, but do you understand the dangers that lurk in the shadows? There are forces at play here that seek to corrupt the magic of this zoo. If you wish to help, you must prove your worth."

Don swallowed hard. "What do I have to do?"

The wolf sat back on its haunches, its glowing eyes never leaving Don's face. "The darkness is spreading. It seeks to claim the creatures of this zoo for its own. You must find the source of this corruption and confront it. But first, you must navigate the trials of the forest. Only then will you earn the right to stand against the shadows."

"What kind of trials?" Don asked, his curiosity piqued.

The wolf stood, its massive form towering over him. "Trials of courage, wit, and heart. You will face what lies within you, and what you fear most. Are you prepared?"

Don felt a mixture of fear and excitement. He had faced challenges before, but nothing quite like this. He nodded, trying to project confidence. "I'm ready."

"Very well," the wolf said, its voice rumbling like distant thunder. "Follow me, and prepare for the first trial."

With that, the wolf turned and led the way deeper into the thicket. The trees closed in around them, the branches intertwining like a woven tapestry. The air grew colder, and a mist rolled in, wrapping around them like a shroud.

"Stay close," the wolf instructed, its ears pricked for any sign of danger. "The trials can distort the path. You may see things that are not there, hear voices that seek to confuse you."

As they moved further into the woods, Don could feel a shift in the atmosphere. The air became thick with a palpable tension, and strange sounds echoed through the trees—whispers that seemed to call his name, laughter that danced just beyond his reach.

"Do not listen to them," the wolf warned, its voice low and steady. "They are illusions designed to distract you. Focus on the path ahead."

Don nodded, trying to push aside the distractions. The glow of his medallion provided a small comfort, illuminating the way forward. As they walked, he began to notice other shapes moving through the trees—dark silhouettes flitting between the branches, their forms indistinct.

"What are those?" Don asked, glancing nervously at the shadows.

"The lost souls of the zoo," the wolf replied. "Creatures who have succumbed to the darkness. They seek to lure others into the shadows. Stay strong, and do not be swayed by their cries."

Just then, they came to a clearing, the moonlight spilling onto the ground like liquid silver. At the center stood a large stone altar, worn and covered in vines. Strange markings were etched into its surface, glowing faintly with an eerie light.

"This is the first trial," the wolf said, pacing around the altar. "You must face the shadows of your past. Touch the altar, and you will be confronted with your greatest fears."

Don hesitated, his heart racing. He had always been afraid of failure, of not being enough. But he had come this far; he couldn't turn back now. Taking a deep breath, he stepped forward and placed his hand on the cool stone.

The moment his palm made contact, the world around him shifted. The clearing faded away, replaced by a swirling darkness. He found himself standing in a familiar place—his old school, but it felt different. The air was thick with tension, and the hallways were eerily quiet.

Suddenly, he was surrounded by shadows—his classmates, their faces twisted in mockery. "Look who it is," one voice sneered. "Don the dreamer. What are you doing here? You'll never be anything."

Don's heart sank. The voices echoed his deepest insecurities, magnifying his fears until they loomed larger than life. He felt small, insignificant, trapped in a nightmare of his own making.

"No!" he shouted, shaking his head. "This isn't real!"

The shadows closed in, whispering words of doubt and despair. "You don't belong here. You never did."

But as they pressed closer, something inside Don ignited. He remembered the adventures he had embarked upon, the challenges he had faced. The friends who believed in him and the courage he had found within himself.

"You're wrong!" he cried, his voice strong. "I am more than my fears. I have a purpose!"

With those words, the shadows recoiled, their forms dissolving into wisps of smoke. The darkness around him began to lighten, and he felt the weight of his insecurities lift.

Suddenly, he was back in the clearing, standing before the wolf, who regarded him with approval. "You have faced your first trial, Don.

But there are more challenges ahead. You must remain vigilant and true to yourself."

Don replied, still feeling the adrenaline coursing through his veins. "What's next?"

"Now, you will face the trial of wit," the wolf said, turning toward the path that led deeper into the woods. "Follow me, and prepare to test your mind against the shadows that seek to deceive you."

Chapter 6: Timmy's Encounter with the Trickster Monkeys

Unlike his friends, Timmy had always been more cautious, often hesitant to jump into the unknown. But tonight felt different. The air buzzed with energy, and the whispers of the night seemed to call him deeper into the zoo.

The trees on either side grew denser, their trunks twisted and gnarled, stretching toward the sky like ancient giants. Shadows flickered in the corners of his vision, but he didn't dare look back. The deeper he went, the more he could sense the magic pulsing in the air. With each step, he could feel a strange combination of fear and excitement brewing in his chest.

After a few minutes of walking, Timmy stumbled into a clearing. In the center stood a colorful sign that read, "Monkey Mischief Exhibit." Beneath it, a large wooden gate was slightly ajar, swinging gently in the night breeze. Intrigued, Timmy approached, peering through the gap. The sound of chattering filled the air—loud, boisterous, and undeniably playful.

"Maybe I should check it out," he murmured to himself, a mix of curiosity and apprehension swirling within him. Gathering his courage, he pushed the gate open and stepped inside.

The enclosure was vibrant, filled with tropical plants and vines, their leaves shimmering under the soft glow of lanterns hanging from the branches. Colorful decorations adorned the area, and he could see monkeys swinging from the branches, their fur a riot of colors—golden, black, and brown. They chattered excitedly, their voices overlapping in a cacophony of sound.

Timmy couldn't help but smile. He had always loved monkeys—their playful antics and boundless energy captivated him. But as he ventured further into the exhibit, he realized these monkeys were different. Their eyes sparkled with mischief, and there was an unmistakable glint of cunning in their expressions.

"Hey there, little guys!" Timmy called, waving at them. "What's all the fuss about?"

As if in response, a particularly cheeky monkey swung down from a branch and landed in front of him. It was small, with bright green eyes and an enormous grin that stretched from ear to ear. The monkey tilted its head, studying Timmy with a playful gaze.

"Welcome, welcome!" the monkey chirped, its voice high-pitched and animated. "I'm Tiko, the king of mischief! What brings you to our jungle?"

Timmy chuckled at the monkey's enthusiastic demeanor. "I'm Timmy! I'm here for an adventure. My friends and I are exploring the zoo tonight."

"An adventure, you say?" Tiko's eyes sparkled with mischief. "Well, you've come to the right place! We love a good game around here. But beware, human—if you're going to play with us, you'd better be clever!"

Timmy felt a surge of excitement. "What kind of games?"

"Oh, the best kinds!" Tiko declared, bouncing on his feet. "We play tricks, solve puzzles, and sometimes, we just make a mess! You'll have to prove you're up to the challenge if you want to earn your keep here. Are you ready to test your wits?"

Before Timmy could answer, the other monkeys began to gather around, chattering excitedly. He glanced at them, then back at Tiko, who was looking at him with eager anticipation.

"Alright, I'm in!" Timmy said, determination setting in. "What's the first challenge?"

Tiko clapped his hands together, causing the other monkeys to cheer. "Wonderful! Let's start with a riddle. Solve it, and you'll earn the right to join our mischief! But if you fail... well, you might find yourself in a bit of a sticky situation!"

Timmy raised an eyebrow, intrigued but slightly nervous. "What's the riddle?"

Tiko hopped up onto a nearby branch, his tiny frame silhouetted against the lanterns. "Listen closely! I speak without a mouth and hear without ears. I have no body, but I can still create chaos. What am I?"

Timmy furrowed his brow, his mind racing. It sounded like a classic riddle, but he couldn't quite place it. The monkeys watched him intently, their eyes gleaming with mischief.

"Think, Timmy, think!" he murmured to himself. He pictured the words in his mind, dissecting them. *Speak without a mouth... hear without ears... create chaos...*

Suddenly, it hit him. "An echo!" he exclaimed, feeling a rush of triumph. "The answer is an echo!"

Tiko clapped his hands, clearly impressed. "Brilliant! You've got the brain of a monkey! Now, for your next challenge..."

Timmy grinned, feeling a surge of confidence. "What's next?"

Tiko pointed to a large pile of brightly colored balls scattered across the ground. "You must gather all the balls and place them in the correct colors before the timer runs out! But beware—my friends here will try to distract you!"

Before he could respond, a chorus of excited chattering erupted from the monkeys. They scattered around the clearing, ready to create chaos. Tiko stepped back, a gleam in his eye. "You have five minutes! Go!"

Timmy wasted no time. He dashed toward the pile of balls, each one a vibrant hue—red, blue, yellow, and green. He quickly began sorting them, throwing the red ones to one side, then the blue, working as fast as he could.

The monkeys, however, had other plans. They swooped down from the trees, grabbing balls and tossing them into the air. A few cheeky ones even rolled on the ground, snatching the balls back as Timmy tried to pick them up.

"Hey! Come on!" Timmy laughed, trying to dodge a mischievous monkey that was now attempting to steal a bright yellow ball from his hands.

As he focused on gathering the balls, he realized he had to outsmart them. Instead of getting frustrated, he decided to use their energy against them. "Alright, you little tricksters," he said, smirking. "How about a game?"

He held up a bright blue ball. "If you can catch this ball before I throw it, you can have it!"

The monkeys paused, their eyes widening with excitement. They loved a good chase. With a flick of his wrist, Timmy tossed the ball into the air, and the monkeys darted after it, screeching in delight.

Quickly, Timmy used the distraction to scoop up the remaining balls. He raced to the designated area, where he arranged them by color, his heart pounding in rhythm with the ticking timer.

Just as he finished placing the last ball, Tiko shouted, "Time's up!"

Panting and exhilarated, Timmy turned to see Tiko inspecting the colorful arrangement. "Well done, Timmy! You've passed the trial of wit!"

The other monkeys clapped and cheered, their chattering filling the air with laughter. Timmy couldn't help but grin, his heart swelling with pride.

"Now, for the final challenge," Tiko announced, settling back on a branch. "This one will test your heart! Follow me!"

The monkeys led him deeper into the exhibit, through twisting vines and hanging ropes, until they reached a tall tree with a sturdy trunk. At the top, a rickety wooden platform swayed in the breeze.

"Up there lies your next challenge," Tiko explained, gesturing toward the platform. "You must climb to the top and retrieve the golden banana. It's a symbol of trust and friendship in our world."

Timmy looked up at the platform, swallowing hard. Heights had never been his strong suit. "What if I fall?"

Tiko gave him an encouraging smile. "You'll have your friends below to catch you. Trust in your heart, Timmy!"

Taking a deep breath, Timmy nodded. He stepped forward, gripping the rough bark of the tree as he began to climb. Each branch felt sturdy beneath his hands, but as he climbed higher, the ground below shrank away, and a wave of vertigo washed over him.

"Just focus on the goal!" he whispered to himself, pushing through his fear. "You can do this!"

Finally, he reached the platform. It swayed beneath him, and he knelt down, scanning the surface for the golden banana. And there it was, shining brightly, its color glowing even in the dim light. He grabbed it, feeling its warmth radiate through his fingers.

Just as he turned to climb back down, the platform swayed again, causing him to stumble. "Whoa!" he shouted, flailing to regain his balance.

"Timmy!" the monkeys called from below, their voices a mix of concern and excitement. "You've got this!"

Taking a deep breath, he steadied himself. "I'm alright!" he called back, summoning every ounce of confidence he had. With the banana securely in hand, he began his descent, careful and deliberate.

When he finally reached the ground, the monkeys erupted into cheers. Tiko hopped down from his perch and clapped Timmy on the shoulder. "You did it! You faced your fears and showed great heart!"

Timmy beamed, holding up the golden banana triumphantly. "I couldn't have done it without you all!"

The monkeys danced around him, their playful energy infectious. "Now, you're one of us!" Tiko exclaimed, his green eyes shining with excitement. "You're ready for whatever lies ahead!"

Feeling a sense of belonging he hadn't expected, Timmy laughed and joined in the celebration. They swung from the branches, tumbled on the grass, and reveled in the joy of the night.

As the festivities began to settle down, Tiko approached Timmy with a more serious expression. "Remember, Timmy, tonight is just the beginning. You have proven your worth, but the darkness is still out there. Stay true to yourself and trust your heart. The path ahead will require all of us."

Timmy nodded, his excitement tempered by the weight of Tiko's words. He glanced around at the jubilant monkeys, grateful for their friendship. "I will. Thank you for believing in me."

. As he prepared to leave the exhibit, Tiko handed him a small trinket—a miniature wooden monkey carved intricately, glowing with a soft light.

"Keep this close," Tiko said. "It will remind you of our friendship and the light that shines within you."

Timmy accepted the gift with a grateful smile, tucking it safely into his pocket. He turned and made his way back to the path, eager to reunite with his friends and share the adventures he had experienced.

Chapter 7: Jake's Escape from the Gargoyle Garden

As Jake made his way along the misty path, he felt a mix of excitement and apprehension. While his friends had been off facing their challenges, he had been left alone to navigate the unknown. He tightened his grip on the glowing stone in his hand, which pulsed softly, illuminating the darkness around him.

The shadows seemed to shift with every step he took, creeping closer and further away, their movements almost teasing him. He had always been one for pranks and mischief, but this felt different. There was an underlying seriousness in the air tonight, a weight that hung over the zoo like a storm cloud waiting to burst.

As he rounded a bend, the trees parted to reveal a sprawling garden filled with intricate stone statues and elaborate gargoyles perched on crumbling pedestals. They stood watch over the garden, their eyes carved into expressions of vigilance and ferocity.

Jake took a deep breath. "Wow, this is kind of creepy," he muttered to himself. The air was thick with the scent of damp earth and moss, and the only sound was the rustling of leaves as the wind whispered through the trees.

At the far end of the garden, an enormous stone gate loomed, its entrance adorned with twisting vines and ominous carvings. The gargoyles seemed to come alive in the moonlight, their stone faces glimmering like ghostly sentinels.

"Guess it's time to see what's behind door number one," Jake said, mustering up his bravado. He stepped forward, feeling a mixture of trepidation and thrill as he approached the gate. Just as he reached out to push it open, he heard a low rumble that sent a shiver down his spine.

"Who dares enter the Gargoyle Garden?" a voice echoed, deep and gravelly.

Jake whipped around, searching for the source of the voice. The gargoyles appeared to be watching him, their eyes glowing eerily. "I-I'm just here to explore!" he stammered, trying to sound confident.

"You seek to explore, yet you tread on sacred ground," the voice boomed again. "Prove your worth, and you may pass. Fail, and you shall remain trapped in the garden for eternity!"

"Great," Jake muttered under his breath. He was no stranger to challenges, but this one felt like it was going to test him in ways he hadn't imagined. "What do I need to do?"

"Face your fears and answer our riddle," the voice declared. "Only then will you earn the right to leave."

Jake took a deep breath, feeling the pulse of the stone in his hand. "Fine. What's the riddle?"

"Listen closely," the voice intoned. "I can be cracked, made, told, and played. What am I?"

Jake furrowed his brow, trying to think. "Cracked, made, told, and played... What could it be?"

He paced back and forth, the gargoyles looming over him. "Come on, think!" he urged himself. "You've got this."

Suddenly, an idea struck him. "A joke! The answer is a joke!"

There was a moment of silence before the gargoyle nearest him chuckled, its stone features softening just a bit. "You are clever, boy. But cleverness alone will not free you. The second trial awaits."

"Great," Jake sighed, his nerves tingling. "What's the second trial?"

"Navigate the labyrinth of stone," the voice replied. "Find your way through without getting lost, or face the consequences."

The stone gate creaked open, revealing a winding path that led into the heart of the garden. As Jake stepped inside, he felt a rush of cool air, and the shadows seemed to pulse with life. The walls of the labyrinth loomed high on either side, covered in creeping vines and flickering lanterns.

"Alright, let's do this," he said, setting off into the labyrinth. The path twisted and turned, the walls closing in around him. He could feel the weight of the stones pressing down, and every sound echoed like a heartbeat in his chest.

After several turns, Jake found himself standing at a crossroads, unsure which way to go. He glanced left and right, trying to remember which path he had just taken. The shadows danced in the corners of his vision, whispering words he couldn't quite make out.

"Stay calm," he whispered to himself. "You've faced tougher challenges than this."

He took the left path and continued forward, but after a few moments, he found himself back at the entrance of the labyrinth. "Seriously?" he exclaimed, frustration creeping into his voice. "This is ridiculous!"

Determined to figure it out, he retraced his steps and took the right path this time. The winding corridors seemed to stretch on forever, and he felt a growing sense of unease. The shadows felt closer, whispering taunts that sent chills down his spine.

"You'll never find your way out," one voice sneered, echoing around him. "You're just a prankster lost in the dark."

Jake clenched his fists, refusing to let the shadows get to him. "I'm not lost! I'm just... taking my time!"

As he pushed forward, he stumbled into a small clearing. In the center stood a tall statue of a gargoyle, its wings unfurled and its eyes glowing. It looked almost regal in its stone form, but Jake felt a strange sense of foreboding.

Suddenly, the gargoyle's eyes flickered to life, and it spoke in a booming voice. "You have trespassed long enough. Answer my riddle, or remain trapped forever!"

Jake's heart raced. "What's the riddle?"

The gargoyle tilted its head. "I am not alive, but I can grow; I don't have lungs, but I need air; I don't have a mouth, but water kills me. What am I?"

"Hmm," Jake pondered, feeling the weight of the riddle. It was tricky, and he could sense the tension in the air. "What can grow without being alive...?"

He paced around the statue, considering each word. "Wait! I know!" he exclaimed suddenly. "It's fire! The answer is fire!"

The gargoyle's eyes gleamed, and it let out a low rumble of approval. "Clever boy. You may pass."

With that, the statue stepped aside, revealing a path that twisted deeper into the labyrinth. Jake took a deep breath, relief flooding through him. He had faced his fears and outsmarted the gargoyles so far, but he knew the night was far from over.

As he ventured deeper into the maze, the shadows began to shift around him, the path becoming less defined. Jake could feel his heart racing again, but he pressed on, determined to find his way out.

Finally, after what felt like an eternity, he reached another clearing. This one was bathed in moonlight, and at its center stood a beautiful fountain, its waters sparkling like diamonds. The gargoyles flanked the fountain, their expressions softened by the shimmering light.

Jake approached the fountain cautiously, feeling a strange pull toward it. As he neared the edge, he noticed something floating in the water—a small, glowing stone that mirrored the one in his hand. "What is that?" he murmured, bending down to take a closer look.

Just then, the gargoyles shifted, their eyes narrowing. "Do not touch the waters!" one of them warned, its voice echoing ominously. "You may find what you seek, but you will also unleash what lies beneath."

Jake hesitated, glancing from the stone to the gargoyles. "What do you mean?"

"Some treasures come at a cost," the gargoyle replied cryptically. "What do you value most? Are you willing to sacrifice it?"

Jake took a step back, considering the implications. He had come so far, faced so many challenges, but what was he willing to give up?

His mind raced with thoughts of his friends, the adventures they had shared, and the bonds they had formed. "I don't want to lose anything," he declared, standing tall. "I've already faced my fears tonight. I won't let anything take that away from me!"

With that, he turned and backed away from the fountain, leaving the glowing stone untouched. The gargoyles seemed to nod in approval, and the air shifted, lightening as if a weight had been lifted.

"Wise choice," one of them said. "You have proven your worth, Jake. Now, you may leave the garden."

The stone gate swung open, revealing the path that would lead him back to his friends.

Chapter 8: The Pumpkin Patch Puzzle

Mandy's heart raced as she left the ethereal giraffes behind, clutching the crescent pendant that now hung around her neck. The glow from the pendant provided a reassuring warmth against the chill of the night air. She felt invigorated after her encounter, but the weight of her newfound responsibility loomed large. As she continued down the winding path, she couldn't shake the feeling that she was being watched.

The trees around her grew denser, their branches intertwining like fingers grasping for the sky. Just ahead, a flickering light caught her attention, shimmering through the darkness like a beacon. Drawn to it, she quickened her pace, eager to see what lay ahead.

As she pushed through the underbrush, the path opened into a wide, colorful clearing. Before her lay an expansive pumpkin patch, illuminated by soft, glowing orbs that floated above the pumpkins, casting a magical light across the scene. The pumpkins varied in size, shape, and color—some were bright orange, while others glowed a vivid green or deep purple.

Mandy couldn't help but smile. It was enchanting—like stepping into a dream. She stepped closer, fascinated by the shimmering pumpkins that seemed to pulse with their own light. Each pumpkin bore intricate designs carved into their skins, and many of them seemed to whisper secrets as she passed.

"Welcome to the Pumpkin Patch of Wonders!" a cheerful voice called out.

Mandy turned to see a lively figure bouncing toward her. It was a small, plump fairy, her wings shimmering like the surface of a calm lake. She wore a dress made of pumpkin vines and flower petals, and her hair was a wild tangle of leaves and bright flowers.

"I'm Pippa, the guardian of this patch! What brings you to our magical haven?" the fairy asked, her eyes twinkling with mischief.

"I'm Mandy!" she replied, still entranced by the magical sight. "I'm exploring the zoo tonight. I just came from the giraffes—"

"Ah, the ghostly giraffes! They're quite the sight!" Pippa interrupted with a giggle. "But I sense you're looking for something more. Are you ready for a challenge?"

Mandy's heart raced with anticipation. "What kind of challenge?"

Pippa flitted closer, gesturing to the patch. "This pumpkin patch holds many secrets, and I've hidden a magical treasure within. But to find it, you must solve the Pumpkin Puzzle! Each pumpkin has a riddle carved into its skin, and only by answering correctly will you unlock the next clue."

"Count me in!" Mandy exclaimed, excitement bubbling inside her. She loved puzzles and riddles, especially if they were wrapped in a layer of magic.

"Wonderful!" Pippa clapped her hands, and the glowing orbs above brightened. "But be warned—some riddles are tricky! Choose wisely, and trust your instincts."

Mandy stepped into the patch, the soft earth squishing beneath her feet. She approached the nearest pumpkin, its surface smooth and warm to the touch. The carving glowed faintly, and as she leaned in, the words became clear:

I speak without a mouth and hear without ears. I have no body, but I can still create chaos. What am I?

A familiar riddle—she had heard it before. "An echo!" she called out confidently.

At her answer, the pumpkin shimmered and vibrated, glowing brighter before suddenly splitting open to reveal a small, glowing seed inside. Pippa clapped her hands excitedly. "Correct! One step closer to your treasure!"

Mandy's excitement grew as she continued through the patch, solving riddle after riddle. Each time she answered correctly, another pumpkin would burst open, revealing glowing seeds that danced around her like fireflies.

The next pumpkin read:

I can fly without wings. I can cry without eyes. Whenever I go, darkness flies. What am I?

Mandy thought hard. "A cloud! It can move through the sky and bring rain!"

The pumpkin glowed, and she felt a rush of energy as it burst open, revealing another seed. She gathered it, feeling the warmth radiate from it.

As she moved to the next pumpkin, the riddles became more challenging. One read:

I am taken from a mine, and shut up in a wooden case, from which I am never released. What am I?

After a moment of contemplation, she answered, "Pencil lead!"

The pumpkin exploded into a shower of light, and another seed floated into her hands. The thrill of the hunt invigorated her, but just as she was about to move on, the air shifted.

Mandy noticed a dark shadow creeping across the patch, darkening the glowing orbs. The once-cheerful atmosphere turned tense as the fairy Pippa's smile faltered. "Beware, Mandy! The darkness is near."

"What do you mean?" Mandy asked, her heart pounding.

"The patch is alive with magic, but it can also attract unwanted attention," Pippa explained. "If you don't solve the final puzzle soon, the dark forces will take what you've gathered!"

Determined, Mandy pushed forward, racing from pumpkin to pumpkin, her heart racing. But the next riddle proved to be the toughest yet:

I have lakes with no water, mountains with no stone, and cities with no buildings. What am I?

Mandy bit her lip, her mind racing. She felt the pressure of the looming darkness pressing against her. She had seen this riddle before in a book and knew it had a simple answer, yet it eluded her.

Suddenly, a chilling wind swept through the pumpkin patch, and the shadows began to twist ominously. Panic bubbled inside her. "Come on, think!" she urged herself, pacing back and forth.

Just then, a thought struck her. "A map!" she exclaimed. "It has everything without being a real place!"

The moment she said it, the pumpkin erupted in a dazzling display of light, revealing the last glowing seed. As it floated into her hand, the shadows began to retreat, shrieking in frustration.

"You did it!" Pippa cheered, her wings fluttering in delight. "You've completed the Pumpkin Puzzle! Now, gather the seeds, for they hold great power."

Mandy glanced at the seeds glowing brightly in her hands, feeling a rush of accomplishment. "What do I do with them?"

"The seeds will guide you on your journey," Pippa explained. "Plant them in the ground where you need to find strength. They'll grow into magical vines that will help you when the darkness returns."

Chapter 9: Don's Trial of Wit

The moon hung high overhead, casting an ethereal glow that danced across the trees. Don clutched the Medallion of the Bat tightly, its warmth a comforting reminder of his encounter with Barnaby. But as he moved deeper into the woods, he could feel the atmosphere change—an invisible tension crackled in the air, heavy with uncertainty.

After what felt like an eternity of wandering, the path opened up to a wide, moonlit clearing. In the center stood a large stone pedestal, worn and ancient, with intricate carvings spiraling down its sides. Around the pedestal were seven stone gargoyles, each one uniquely designed—some with fierce expressions, others with more whimsical features. They loomed over the clearing like sentinels guarding a sacred treasure.

"Ah, another brave soul has arrived," one of the gargoyles croaked, its voice gravelly and deep. "Welcome, seeker of knowledge! You stand before the Trial of Wit, a test for those who wish to continue their journey."

Don felt a thrill of both excitement and apprehension. "What do I have to do?" he asked, stepping closer to the pedestal.

The gargoyle closest to him, with its wings folded tightly against its body, grinned widely. "You must answer our riddles! For each one you answer correctly, a path will be revealed. But answer incorrectly, and you will face the consequences."

"Consequences?" Don echoed, a knot tightening in his stomach.

"Fear not! The consequences are simply a bit of mischief," the gargoyle replied with a wink. "But be prepared. Our riddles are crafted to challenge even the sharpest of minds!"

Don took a deep breath, steeling himself for what lay ahead. "Alright, I'm ready. What's the first riddle?"

The gargoyles exchanged glances, their eyes gleaming with excitement. The same gargoyle that had spoken before stepped forward. "Very well. Listen closely:

I have keys but open no locks. I have space but no room. You can enter, but you can't go outside. What am I?"

Don furrowed his brow, mulling over the riddle. *Keys, space, entering but not going outside...* His mind raced through possibilities, but nothing seemed to fit.

"Come on, think!" he urged himself, pacing in a small circle. "Keys... no locks. What could it be?"

Then it clicked. "A piano! The answer is a piano!" he declared, a surge of confidence rushing through him.

The gargoyles erupted in laughter, their voices echoing in the night. "Correct! You have solved the first riddle!" The stone pedestal glowed brightly, and a small path revealed itself behind the gargoyles.

Feeling a wave of relief wash over him, Don prepared for the next challenge. "What's the next riddle?" he asked eagerly.

One of the other gargoyles, with a mischievous twinkle in its eye, stepped forward. "Listen well! Here it is:

The more you take, the more you leave behind. What am I?"

Don thought hard, trying to visualize the riddle. "The more you take... what could that mean?"

He paced again, mulling over the possibilities. Then it dawned on him. "Footsteps! The answer is footsteps!"

The gargoyles cheered once more, their voices blending in a triumphant chorus. "Well done, clever one! You have passed the second test!"

With the second riddle solved, a second path opened, leading deeper into the clearing. Don's heart raced with excitement, but he knew he had to remain focused. The third riddle loomed ahead, and he had no intention of failing.

The tallest gargoyle, with a stern expression, stepped forward, its voice deep and commanding. "Prepare yourself! Here comes the final riddle:

I am always hungry, I must always be fed. The finger I touch will soon turn red. What am I?"

Don felt a rush of urgency. This one was tricky. He thought of all the possibilities, running through various options in his mind. "Always hungry... must be fed..."

After a moment of contemplation, a realization struck him. "Fire! The answer is fire!" he exclaimed.

The gargoyles erupted in cheers, their joy palpable. "Incredible! You have solved all our riddles! You possess the wit required to continue your journey!"

With that, the pedestal glowed brightly, illuminating the paths that lay ahead. The gargoyles stepped aside, revealing a vibrant trail lined with glowing flowers and shimmering stones.

Don felt a rush of accomplishment. He had faced the Trial of Wit and emerged victorious! But just as he was about to step onto the new path, he noticed something moving in the shadows behind the gargoyles.

Before he could react, a dark figure lunged out from the darkness, a shadowy creature with piercing eyes. It snarled, baring sharp teeth, and Don instinctively took a step back, heart racing.

"Who dares to interfere?" one of the gargoyles shouted, its voice filled with authority.

The creature hissed, eyes glinting like embers in the night. "I am here for the light you possess!" It lunged toward Don, who quickly raised the Medallion of the Bat.

The moment he held it up, a radiant light burst forth, pushing back the shadows. The creature recoiled, snarling in frustration. "You think your light can save you? The darkness will always return!"

Don's pulse quickened as he felt the energy of the medallion surge through him. "I won't let it!" he shouted defiantly. "You can't take this magic from me!"

With that declaration, the medallion glowed even brighter, sending out waves of light that pushed back the dark creature. It howled in anger, retreating into the shadows, but not before leaving a lingering sense of dread.

The gargoyles turned to Don, their expressions a mix of concern and admiration. "You have shown great bravery, young one. The darkness will always seek to claim what it cannot have, but you must remain vigilant."

"I will," Don replied, taking a deep breath to steady himself. "I won't let it win."

With that resolve, he stepped onto the path revealed by the gargoyles, feeling the light of the medallion guiding him forward. The world around him began to shift, the clearing fading as he ventured deeper into the unknown.

As he walked, he couldn't shake the image of the dark creature from his mind. It had seemed powerful, and its words echoed ominously in his thoughts. But he refused to let fear take hold. He was on a mission to protect the magic of the zoo, and he would do whatever it took.

The path twisted and turned, leading him through the woods until he finally emerged into another clearing. This one was different—brightly colored lights hung from the trees, illuminating a gathering of animals and creatures of all kinds.

Mandy, Timmy, and Jake were already there, their eyes lighting up as they spotted him.

Chapter 10: The Haunted Aquarium

Timmy's heart raced as he left the pumpkin patch behind, the warmth of the glowing seeds nestled safely in his pocket. He had faced challenges unlike any he had experienced before, and with each riddle he solved, he felt more empowered. But he was eager to reunite with his friends and share what he had learned. The magical energy in the air buzzed around him, heightening his senses as he navigated the winding paths of the zoo.

After walking for a while, Timmy found himself drawn toward a distant glow shimmering through the trees. Curious, he followed the light, pushing aside the branches that obscured his view. As he emerged into another clearing, he gasped at the sight before him.

The entrance to the aquarium stood majestically, its large glass panels reflecting the moonlight. Water flowed gracefully in a stream nearby, its surface shimmering with silver. Colorful lanterns shaped like fish hung from the trees, casting playful shadows on the ground. The atmosphere was enchanting, yet an eerie chill hung in the air.

"Wow, this place looks incredible!" Timmy marveled, stepping closer to the entrance.

As he approached, the glass doors slid open with a gentle whoosh, welcoming him inside. The interior was a kaleidoscope of colors—vibrant fish darted through crystal-clear tanks, while glowing jellyfish floated lazily above. Bioluminescent corals adorned the walls, illuminating the space with a soft, ethereal glow.

However, something felt off. The air was thick with tension, and he could hear faint whispers that seemed to echo through the corridors of the aquarium. The further he ventured in, the more he sensed that something wasn't quite right.

"Hello?" Timmy called out, his voice echoing softly. "Is anyone here?"

A flicker of movement caught his eye, and he turned to see a figure emerge from the shadows. It was a tall, graceful woman with flowing blue hair and shimmering skin that seemed to reflect the colors of the ocean. She wore a dress made of flowing waves, and her eyes glimmered like the depths of the sea.

"Welcome to the Haunted Aquarium," she said, her voice melodic yet haunting. "I am Marina, guardian of these waters. You have entered a realm of magic and mystery, but be warned: this place holds secrets that may not be ready to reveal themselves."

Timmy stepped back slightly, a mixture of awe and unease washing over him. "I'm Timmy. I'm exploring the zoo tonight with my friends. I've already faced a few challenges."

Marina smiled, a glimmer of admiration in her eyes. "You are brave to venture here. The aquarium is home to creatures that thrive in both light and shadow. But there is a darkness that seeks to consume this place. If you wish to help, you must face the Trial of the Waters."

"What does that involve?" Timmy asked, curiosity piqued despite his nerves.

"You will enter the depths of the aquarium, where the shadows dwell," Marina explained. "There, you must navigate through the currents and solve the puzzles that lie beneath the surface. Only by embracing both light and dark will you find the key to overcoming the trials ahead."

Timmy swallowed hard, but a spark of determination ignited within him. He had faced his fears before, and he would do it again. "I'm ready," he said firmly.

Marina led him to a spiral staircase that descended into the depths of the aquarium. The air grew cooler, and the light dimmed as they ventured down. Timmy could hear the sounds of water bubbling and echoing in the distance, and with each step, the whispers grew louder.

As they reached the bottom, Timmy found himself in a large, cavernous room filled with shimmering water tanks. The colors danced around him, and strange creatures glided through the water, their forms both beautiful and eerie.

"Your trial begins now," Marina said, gesturing to a large tank at the center of the room. "You must dive into the depths and retrieve the pearl of wisdom. But beware—the shadows within the water are not what they seem."

Timmy took a deep breath, feeling a rush of excitement mixed with apprehension. He stepped closer to the tank, the water swirling gently as if inviting him in. The surface shimmered, and he could see shadows moving beneath the waves.

Without hesitation, Timmy plunged into the tank. The cool water enveloped him, and he felt a rush of adrenaline as he descended. The light from above faded, replaced by a magical glow emanating from the walls of the tank.

As he swam deeper, the whispers grew louder, echoing around him. "Turn back! You don't belong here!" they taunted, sending shivers down his spine.

"No! I'm not afraid!" he shouted, forcing himself to push through the shadows. He focused on the glow ahead, determined to find the pearl.

Suddenly, dark shapes darted around him—shadowy figures that twisted and turned like tendrils of smoke. Timmy's heart raced as they swirled closer, their whispers growing more frantic. "You'll never escape! This is where you belong!"

But he remembered Marina's words: embrace both light and dark. Timmy took a deep breath, calming himself. He reached out, willing the darkness to reveal itself.

"Show me the truth!" he declared, his voice steady against the chaos.

The shadows paused, swirling around him before slowly transforming into shimmering forms—beautiful fish and graceful sea creatures. The water began to clear, and in the center of the tank, Timmy spotted the pearl glowing softly.

With renewed determination, he swam toward it, his heart pounding with each stroke. He reached out, fingers brushing against the smooth surface of the pearl. Just as he grasped it, the shadows surged, pulling him back with a force that threatened to drag him into the depths.

"No!" Timmy shouted, fighting against the current. He focused on the pearl, feeling its warmth radiate through him. "I will not be afraid!"

Drawing on the energy of the pearl, he pushed against the darkness, breaking free of its grasp. With a surge of strength, he swam toward the surface, bursting out of the tank and gasping for air.

Timmy clutched the pearl tightly, feeling its power coursing through him. As he emerged from the tank, Marina stood waiting, her expression a mix of pride and relief.

Chapter 11: The Enchanted Carousel

Jake emerged from the shadows of the Gargoyle Garden, his heart still racing from the challenges he had faced. The night air was crisp, filled with the sounds of nocturnal creatures and the distant rustle of leaves. He felt a sense of pride swelling within him. He had navigated the labyrinth, solved riddles, and confronted dark forces. Now, he was eager to reunite with his friends and share the experience.

As he continued along the winding path, the trees parted to reveal another clearing bathed in moonlight. At the center stood a whimsical carousel, its vibrant colors glowing against the darkness. The carousel spun slowly, adorned with fantastical creatures—unicorns, dragons, and even a phoenix—each one painted in dazzling hues and intricately detailed.

"Wow, this looks amazing!" Jake exclaimed, a grin spreading across his face. He approached the carousel, captivated by its charm. The sounds of cheerful music floated through the air, inviting him closer.

As he stepped onto the platform, he noticed that the carousel wasn't just beautiful—it was alive. The creatures shifted and swayed, their eyes sparkling with mischief. Jake climbed onto the back of a magnificent dragon, its scales shimmering like precious gems.

"Welcome, brave traveler!" a voice called out. Jake turned to see a striking figure stepping out from the shadows—a tall woman draped in flowing fabric that seemed to ripple like water. Her hair cascaded down her shoulders, adorned with twinkling stars and colorful feathers.

"I am Seraphina, the Keeper of the Enchanted Carousel," she said with a warm smile. "You have arrived at a magical gathering! Would you care to join us in a ride?"

"Absolutely!" Jake replied, excitement bubbling within him. He could feel the energy of the carousel pulsating beneath him, the thrill of adventure urging him to take part in whatever magic awaited.

With a wave of her hand, Seraphina set the carousel spinning faster, and the music grew louder, filling the air with a lively melody. The creatures on the carousel came to life, galloping and soaring as if they were in a race.

"Hold on tight!" Seraphina warned, her laughter ringing out like chimes.

Jake felt the wind whip through his hair as the carousel spun faster, the colors blurring into a vibrant whirlwind. He could hardly contain his joy, laughing as the dragon beneath him spread its wings and soared above the ground.

But as the ride continued, the atmosphere began to shift. The once-cheerful music grew darker, and Jake could feel the shadows creeping closer, wrapping around the edges of the carousel. The vibrant colors dulled, and the creatures' expressions shifted from playful to sinister.

"Something's not right," Jake shouted over the music, gripping the dragon tightly. "What's happening?"

Seraphina's expression changed, her brow furrowing in concern. "The carousel draws power from the magic of this zoo, but dark forces seek to corrupt it. You must face the challenge to restore the balance!"

"What do I need to do?" Jake asked, adrenaline coursing through him.

"The carousel holds secrets," Seraphina explained urgently. "You must ride the creatures and answer their riddles to break the spell. Only then can you restore the light!"

Jake nodded, determination surging within him. He took a deep breath, focusing on the task at hand. The dragon beneath him swirled in place, its eyes locked onto his.

"Alright! Let's do this!" he called out.

As the carousel continued to spin, the creatures began to recite their riddles, each one a test of Jake's wit. The first creature, a gallant unicorn, leaned down and spoke in a melodic voice:

I can run but never walk. I have a mouth but never talk. What am I?

"Hmm..." Jake pondered, feeling the thrill of the challenge. "A river! The answer is a river!"

The unicorn neighed joyfully, and a burst of light erupted from its horn, illuminating the carousel momentarily. The shadows receded, and Jake felt a surge of hope.

The next creature, a majestic phoenix, took its turn. "Here is my riddle:

What begins with T, ends with T, and has T in it?"

Jake furrowed his brow, thinking hard. *T, T, and T...* And then it clicked. "A teapot! The answer is a teapot!"

The phoenix flapped its wings, releasing a shower of sparkling feathers that scattered into the air. The carousel brightened, and the shadows continued to retreat.

Feeling emboldened, Jake prepared for the next riddle. A fearsome dragon with emerald scales stepped forward, its voice deep and rumbling.

I fly without wings. I cry without eyes. Whenever I go, darkness flies. What am I?

Jake's mind raced. This riddle sounded familiar, but he couldn't quite place it. As he wrestled with the answer, he noticed the shadows creeping closer, their whispers growing louder.

"I won't let you win!" he shouted defiantly, focusing on the dragon. "I know this one! It's a cloud! The answer is a cloud!"

The dragon roared in approval, its scales shimmering brightly. With each correct answer, Jake felt the shadows retreating further, the carousel glowing with renewed energy.

"Keep going, Jake!" Seraphina encouraged. "You're almost there!"

Just as he was about to move on, a deep rumble echoed through the carousel, and the final creature emerged—a gargantuan beast with a lion's body and the wings of an eagle. Its eyes glinted with challenge as it spoke.

I am taken from a mine, and shut up in a wooden case, from which I am never released. What am I?

Jake's heart raced. He remembered hearing this riddle before but struggled to recall the answer. He could feel the shadows creeping closer, their presence pressing against him.

"Think, think!" he muttered under his breath, recalling the riddle's clues. Then it struck him. "Pencil lead! The answer is pencil lead!"

The creature let out a mighty roar, and a blinding light enveloped the carousel. The shadows shrieked in agony as they were banished, the music swelling in triumph.

With the last riddle solved, the carousel spun faster, the light intensifying until it enveloped Jake completely. When the brightness faded, he found himself standing in the center of the clearing, the carousel silent and still before him.

"Jake!" Seraphina called, rushing over. "You did it! You broke the spell!"

Jake beamed with pride, the adrenaline still coursing through his veins. "I can't believe I actually did it!"

As the echoes of the shadows faded, the carousel transformed, its colors brightening once more. The creatures on it resumed their lively dance, their expressions now joyful and inviting.

"Thank you for your bravery," Seraphina said, her voice filled with gratitude. "The carousel is now free from darkness, thanks to you. Take this as a token of your triumph."

She handed Jake a small, ornate key shaped like a star. "This key will unlock new adventures and help you face the challenges that lie ahead."

Jake accepted the key, feeling its weight in his hand. "Thank you, Seraphina. I couldn't have done it without your guidance."

With a wave of her hand, Seraphina opened a path leading back to the main area of the zoo. "Now go, brave one! Rejoin your friends and continue your journey."

Chapter 12: The Midnight Menagerie

As Jake walked through the illuminated paths of the zoo, the excitement from his encounter at the enchanted carousel still buzzed in his veins. The key he held in his pocket felt warm and alive, almost vibrating with potential. He couldn't wait to share his experience with Don, Mandy, and Timmy. They had each faced their own challenges, and together, they could unlock even more magic.

The path twisted and turned, leading him toward the center of the zoo, where a glowing light beckoned him closer. As he neared, he could make out the familiar figures of his friends gathered in a clearing surrounded by large, colorful tents. The atmosphere was charged with anticipation, and a sense of wonder filled the air.

"Mandy! Timmy! Don!" he called out, waving as he approached.

"Jake!" they all exclaimed, rushing to meet him. "You made it back!"

"Did you face the trial?" Don asked, his eyes gleaming with curiosity.

"I did! It was amazing!" Jake replied, recounting the challenges he faced on the enchanted carousel and the riddles he solved. "And I got this!" He pulled the star-shaped key from his pocket, holding it up for them to see.

"Wow, that's incredible!" Mandy said, her eyes wide with excitement. "We've all had our adventures too. You won't believe what we've discovered."

Timmy chimed in, "This place is full of surprises! But look over there!" He pointed toward the large tents, which seemed to vibrate with energy. "I think we're about to see something special."

The friends made their way toward the tents, their hearts pounding with anticipation. As they drew closer, they noticed colorful banners hanging from the entrance, adorned with whimsical designs of animals and magical creatures. A sign at the front read: *Midnight Menagerie: Enter at Your Own Risk!*

"What does that mean?" Jake wondered aloud, a mix of excitement and caution in his voice.

"Only one way to find out!" Don said, his adventurous spirit shining through.

They stepped inside, and the moment they crossed the threshold, they were enveloped in a world of wonder. The interior was alive with vibrant colors, illuminated by floating lanterns that shimmered like stars. Strange creatures roamed freely among the tents—some familiar, like rabbits and birds, while others were extraordinary hybrids with features that defied description.

"Look at that!" Mandy pointed to a small creature with the body of a cat and the wings of a butterfly flitting about playfully. "It's adorable!"

Jake marveled at the array of creatures, each one more fascinating than the last. The tents were filled with exotic animals, many of which seemed to have a sparkle of magic in their eyes.

Suddenly, a loud voice echoed through the tent, drawing their attention to a raised platform at the center. A tall, mysterious figure dressed in vibrant robes stood proudly, flanked by two shimmering peacocks.

"Welcome, welcome to the Midnight Menagerie!" the figure boomed, their voice rich and resonant. "I am Lucian, the keeper of wonders! Tonight, you will witness feats of magic and experience the extraordinary."

The crowd gathered around the platform, captivated by Lucian's presence. "But first, dear friends, we must know: do you possess the courage to join us in this magical spectacle?"

The friends exchanged glances, the thrill of adventure coursing through them. "We're in!" Don declared, stepping forward.

"Excellent!" Lucian grinned, gesturing toward a grand tent on the other side of the clearing. "But first, you must prove your worth. Each of you will face a trial of your own, a test to determine your bond with the magic that surrounds you. Only then may you join the Midnight Menagerie!"

Timmy felt a thrill of excitement and a hint of nervousness. "What kind of trials?"

Lucian waved his hand, and the tent flaps opened to reveal an array of mystical creatures waiting inside. "Each tent holds a different challenge. Choose wisely, and face what lies within!"

Mandy was the first to step forward, her curiosity piqued. "I'll go first!"

"Brave choice!" Lucian said, a hint of admiration in his voice. "Step into the tent and embrace the challenge that awaits you!"

Mandy took a deep breath and entered the tent, the flaps closing behind her. The friends stood outside, anticipation buzzing in the air as they waited for her to return.

Inside the tent, Mandy found herself in a lush forest filled with vibrant flowers and towering trees. She could hear the sound of chirping birds and rustling leaves, and the air was thick with the scent of blooming petals.

"Welcome, seeker of magic!" a melodic voice called out, and she turned to see a graceful fairy with shimmering wings hovering nearby. "I am Lira, and I will guide you through the Trial of Nature. To pass, you must connect with the elements and summon their power."

"What do I need to do?" Mandy asked, feeling a sense of determination.

"Feel the energy around you," Lira instructed. "Find the three elemental stones hidden within the forest—Earth, Air, and Water. Only by uniting their powers can you complete the trial."

Mandy nodded, and the fairy gestured to the trees. "Your journey begins now!"

With renewed resolve, Mandy set off deeper into the enchanted forest, her senses alive with magic. The vibrant colors of the flowers and the soft glow of the light felt like an extension of herself, guiding her forward.

She searched high and low, exploring nooks and crannies, feeling the earth beneath her feet. After a short while, she discovered a small, moss-covered stone, pulsating with energy.

"This must be the Earth stone!" she exclaimed, holding it up triumphantly.

"Good start!" Lira's voice echoed, encouraging her onward. "But there are two more stones to find."

Mandy pressed on, her determination unwavering. She followed a gentle breeze that whispered through the trees, leading her to a clearing where a shimmering waterfall cascaded down rocks, pooling into a crystal-clear pond.

She spotted a glimmer beneath the surface. "The Water stone!" she shouted, reaching into the cool water and retrieving it. The moment she touched it, a surge of energy flowed through her, connecting her to the essence of the water itself.

"Just one more to go!" she cheered, feeling the weight of the stones in her hands.

As she turned to leave, she felt the wind pick up around her, swirling playfully. "The Air stone must be nearby," she thought, following the breeze as it beckoned her onward.

She followed the path until she arrived at a high cliff overlooking the forest below. The wind roared around her, and she knew this was where the final stone would be.

Mandy took a deep breath and focused, closing her eyes as she extended her hands into the air. "Show me the Air stone!" she called out, channeling her energy.

In response, a swirling vortex of wind formed before her, spiraling and dancing. As the gusts intensified, a small stone began to materialize in the center of the whirlwind. It glowed a soft white, shimmering like the morning sky.

With determination, she reached out and grasped the Air stone as it floated gently into her palm. Instantly, a wave of energy washed over her, uniting her with the elements.

"I have them all!" she exclaimed, holding the three stones high. The ground trembled slightly as the magic of nature responded to her call.

"Now unite them!" Lira's voice urged from somewhere nearby.

Mandy quickly pressed the stones together, feeling their energies intertwine. A brilliant flash of light erupted from the stones, filling the clearing with a radiant glow. The power surged through her, connecting her with the very essence of the earth, air, and water.

As the light faded, she found herself standing back in the tent, the stones now glowing softly in her hands. The friends outside cheered, their faces filled with excitement.

"Did you do it?" Timmy asked eagerly.

"I did! I found all three elemental stones!" Mandy replied, beaming with pride.

"Fantastic!" Don cheered. "You've completed your trial!"

Just then, the tent flaps opened wide, and Lira appeared beside Mandy. "You have proven your connection with nature and the elements, dear one. The magic flows strongly within you. Now, you may join the Midnight Menagerie!"

Mandy joined her friends, their spirits lifted as they reveled in her success. "Who's next?" Jake asked, glancing at the remaining tents.

"I'll go!" Timmy volunteered, stepping forward with determination.

"Very well!" Lucian called, gesturing toward the next tent. "Embrace the challenge that awaits you!"

As Timmy stepped into the tent, Jake turned to Mandy and whispered, "I can't believe how incredible this place is!"

"Right? Each trial seems to reveal more magic than the last!" Mandy replied, her eyes sparkling with excitement.

Inside the tent, Timmy found himself in a dimly lit space filled with shadows. The air felt thick, and a low, rhythmic pulse resonated around him, like the beat of a heart.

"Welcome, brave one!" a deep voice echoed, and Timmy turned to see a towering figure with dark feathers and piercing eyes. "I am Kael, guardian of the Shadows. You stand before the Trial of the Mind. To succeed, you must navigate the labyrinth of your thoughts and confront your greatest fears."

Timmy swallowed hard, feeling a knot of anxiety twist in his stomach. "What do I need to do?"

"Step forward into the darkness," Kael instructed, gesturing to a swirling vortex of shadows that loomed before him. "Face what lies within and emerge unscathed."

Taking a deep breath, Timmy stepped into the shadows. The darkness enveloped him, and he felt disoriented as the world shifted around him.

Images flashed in front of his eyes—memories of times he felt afraid or unsure. He saw himself standing alone, feeling abandoned, and the fear of failure loomed large.

"No!" Timmy shouted, shaking his head. "I'm not afraid!"

As he pushed forward, he was confronted by a reflection of himself, the shadows twisting into a doppelgänger that mirrored his insecurities. "You can't escape me," it hissed, eyes glinting with malice. "You are nothing without your friends."

"I am not nothing!" Timmy replied, his voice steady. "I have courage and strength, and I won't let fear control me!"

The shadowy figure laughed, a chilling sound that echoed around him. "Then prove it! Face the truth of your own limitations!"

Timmy clenched his fists, recalling the challenges he had faced alongside his friends. They had each encountered their fears and overcome them. "I may not be perfect, but I am not defined by my fears!" he declared.

With that proclamation, the shadows began to swirl around him, and the image of his doppelgänger faded, replaced by a beam of light that filled the space with warmth. The labyrinth began to dissolve, and Timmy felt the power of the light surge within him.

Chapter 13: The Final Showdown with Mr. Grimble

The night air was electric with anticipation as Don, Mandy, Timmy, and Jake stood together, their hearts racing in unison. They had faced countless challenges, each one drawing them closer together, sharpening their resolve to protect the magic of the zoo. The Midnight Menagerie had revealed their individual strengths, but now they felt the weight of the darkness looming ahead, ready to confront whatever awaited them.

"Alright, what's our next move?" Don asked, glancing around the gathering area filled with the vibrant creatures they had encountered. "We know there's a threat, and I can feel it in the air."

Mandy nodded, gripping the seeds she had gathered from the pumpkin patch. "I think we need to head toward the heart of the zoo. That's where the magic feels strongest—and where I sensed the darkness earlier."

"Right," Jake said, his eyes narrowing with determination. "Let's stick together. Whatever is out there, we can face it as a team."

Timmy held up the pearl he had retrieved from the Haunted Aquarium. "And we have these magical items to help us. The light will guide us."

With newfound purpose, the friends moved toward the path that led deeper into the zoo. The trees formed a canopy overhead, creating an ethereal tunnel as they ventured further. The atmosphere was thick with magic, but a sense of unease began to settle in as shadows danced in the corners of their vision.

As they walked, the whispers of the shadows grew louder, echoing unsettling thoughts. "You'll never make it," they taunted. "You're just children. What can you do against the darkness?"

But the friends stood tall, united against the voices. "We've already faced so much together," Mandy said confidently. "We won't let fear win!"

At last, they reached a clearing where the trees parted to reveal a large, ancient oak. The ground was covered in shimmering light, and at the base of the tree, a figure stood—Mr. Grimble, the zookeeper.

His expression was twisted with anger, and the shadows coiled around him like living tendrils. "So, you've come to confront me, have you?" he sneered, his voice low and menacing. "You think you can stop me from reclaiming the magic that rightfully belongs to the shadows?"

The friends exchanged glances, fear creeping in, but determination hardened their resolve. "We won't let you take anything from this zoo!" Don shouted, stepping forward. "The magic belongs to everyone, not just to you!"

Mr. Grimble let out a hollow laugh. "You foolish children. You don't understand the power of the darkness! It consumes all, and you will be the first to fall."

Without warning, the shadows surged toward them, writhing like snakes. Don raised the Medallion of the Bat, its light illuminating the clearing. "We're not afraid of you!" he declared, the medallion glowing brighter as he focused on the shadows.

The darkness recoiled momentarily, and Mr. Grimble's expression shifted to one of surprise. "What? How is this possible?"

"Because we believe in the magic of this zoo!" Mandy shouted, her voice strong and unwavering. She stepped forward, the seeds from the pumpkin patch glowing in her hands. "And we won't let you take it away!"

With a wave of her hand, she scattered the seeds into the air, and they erupted into vibrant vines that wrapped around the shadows, binding them in place. The vines glowed with a radiant light, pushing back against the darkness.

"Impossible!" Mr. Grimble shouted, struggling against the restraints. "You think you can defeat me with such trivial magic?"

"Trivial?" Timmy exclaimed, stepping up beside Mandy. "This magic represents hope, courage, and friendship! And that's more powerful than any darkness!"

Jake held up the star-shaped key. "And we're not done yet!" With a determined thrust, he unlocked the energy within himself, channeling it through the key. A beam of light shot out, striking the base of the ancient oak tree.

The ground trembled, and the light burst forth in a dazzling display, illuminating the entire clearing. The shadows shrieked in fury, retreating from the radiant energy that surged through the air.

"Keep pushing!" Don shouted, encouraging his friends to channel their energies together. "We can do this!"

With renewed strength, they focused their powers, forming a circle around Mr. Grimble, who was still ensnared by the glowing vines. The shadows writhed and twisted, but the light only grew stronger.

Suddenly, a low growl echoed from behind them. The friends turned to see a pack of spectral wolves emerging from the shadows, their eyes gleaming like stars in the night sky. They stood protectively between the children and Mr. Grimble, their forms shifting between light and shadow.

"You dare to summon the wolves against me?" Mr. Grimble snarled, his anger boiling over. "You think their loyalty will save you?"

The lead wolf stepped forward, its voice resonating like thunder. "We are the guardians of this zoo, bound by the magic that flows through it. We will not allow the darkness to consume our home."

With that declaration, the wolves lunged toward Mr. Grimble, their forms swirling with energy. The shadows twisted violently, but the combined strength of the wolves and the friends pushed back against the darkness, creating a barrier of light.

"Stay strong!" Jake shouted, feeling the energy from the key surging through him. "Together, we can defeat him!"

As the shadows collided with the wolves, the clearing erupted into chaos—light and dark swirling in a breathtaking dance of magic. The ground trembled beneath them, but the bonds of friendship and courage held strong.

With a final surge of determination, the friends channeled their powers into one concentrated blast of light, aimed directly at Mr. Grimble. "We won't let you win!" they shouted in unison.

The light erupted from their hands, a brilliant beam of magic that pierced through the shadows, striking Mr. Grimble squarely in the chest. He howled in rage, the shadows writhing around him as he struggled to hold on to the darkness.

But the power of their friendship overwhelmed him, and with a final cry, the shadows began to dissolve, retreating into the darkness from which they came. The ground shook violently, and the light enveloped Mr. Grimble, consuming him until he was gone.

As the last remnants of darkness faded away, a profound silence filled the clearing. The spectral wolves stood tall and proud, their forms glowing with a gentle light. The friends looked around, their hearts racing with disbelief and joy.

Chapter 14: The Celebration of Lights

The air was filled with the sounds of laughter and music as Don, Mandy, Timmy, and Jake stepped into the gathering area at the heart of the zoo. The clearing was transformed, awash in a kaleidoscope of colors, illuminated by twinkling lights that floated like stars above. Creatures of all shapes and sizes mingled, celebrating the victory over darkness with a joyful exuberance that was infectious.

"Look at this place!" Jake exclaimed, his eyes wide with wonder. "It's incredible!"

Mandy smiled, her heart swelling with pride. "We did it! We really did it!"

As they walked further into the clearing, they were greeted by friendly faces—animals and magical creatures alike, all gathering to honor the heroes who had protected their home. A giant tortoise wearing a colorful garland approached them, its voice deep and wise.

"Thank you, brave children," it said, bowing its head slightly. "You have restored the light to our zoo and protected us from the shadows. Tonight, we celebrate your courage!"

The friends exchanged glances, their hearts racing with joy. "We couldn't have done it without everyone's help," Don said, stepping forward. "This victory belongs to all of us."

The tortoise nodded in appreciation. "Your humility speaks volumes. Come! Join us in the celebration!"

They followed the tortoise into the heart of the festivities, where a long table was laid out with an array of delicious foods—fruits that sparkled like jewels, cakes that glimmered in every color of the rainbow, and sweet pastries that filled the air with enticing aromas.

"Wow, this looks amazing!" Timmy exclaimed, his eyes lighting up as he grabbed a slice of sparkling cake.

"Don't fill up too quickly!" Mandy warned with a grin. "We want to enjoy everything."

As they feasted, laughter filled the air, and stories of their adventures were exchanged. Creatures shared tales of how the shadows had affected their lives, and everyone expressed their gratitude for the friends' bravery.

"Did you see the way you faced those shadows?" a talking parrot squawked, flapping its colorful wings. "You showed them who's boss!"

Jake laughed, feeling a warm glow of camaraderie. "We couldn't have done it without each other. Each of us brought something special to the table."

Once the feast had concluded, Seraphina, the Keeper of the Enchanted Carousel, stepped forward to address the crowd. "Tonight is a night of celebration, not only for the victory over darkness but for the bond forged among friends," she declared, her voice ringing clear.

The crowd erupted in cheers, and the friends felt a swell of pride. They had faced the darkness together, and now they were stronger for it.

"To honor our brave heroes, we will now light the Lanterns of Hope!" Seraphina continued. "Each lantern represents a wish, a dream, or a promise for the future!"

The friends watched as creatures of all kinds gathered around a large bonfire, where dozens of beautiful lanterns were placed. Each lantern was adorned with unique designs, and the magic of the zoo glimmered within them.

"Make a wish," Jake said, glancing at his friends. "Let's make sure we protect this magic forever."

Mandy nodded, her eyes bright. "Let's promise to stick together, no matter what challenges come our way."

Don took a deep breath, thinking of all the adventures they had shared. "I wish for our friendship to always be strong, and for us to always find the light, even in the darkest times."

Timmy smiled, feeling a sense of hope wash over him. "And I wish for everyone here to continue believing in the magic of the zoo. Together, we can overcome anything!"

As they voiced their wishes, Seraphina raised her arms, signaling the start of the lantern-lighting ceremony. One by one, the creatures took their lanterns and released them into the night sky. The lanterns floated upward, illuminating the dark with their warm glow.

Jake felt a sense of awe as he watched the lanterns drift higher and higher, sparkling like stars in the night. "This is beautiful," he said softly, feeling the magic of the moment wash over him.

As the last lantern ascended, a hush fell over the crowd. The night sky was alive with glowing lights, each one representing a wish and a promise. In that moment, they were united, a community bound by their hopes and dreams.

Just then, a soft voice broke the silence. "And now, let us dance!" Marina, the guardian of the Haunted Aquarium, floated forward, her presence radiant and captivating.

The music swelled, and creatures of all shapes and sizes began to dance, their movements fluid and graceful. The friends exchanged excited glances and joined in, laughter filling the air as they moved to the rhythm of the enchanting melody.

Don found himself twirling Mandy around, while Jake and Timmy attempted to keep up with a group of cheerful fairies flitting about. "This is incredible!" Timmy shouted, trying to catch his breath amid the fun.

As the night wore on, they danced under the glowing lanterns, surrounded by friends and creatures who celebrated the magic of the zoo. The shadows had been banished, and for now, joy reigned supreme.

After what felt like hours, the friends gathered together, breathless and exhilarated. "I can't remember the last time I had this much fun," Jake said, his face glowing with happiness.

"Neither can I," Mandy replied, her heart full. "This night has been unforgettable!"

As the celebrations continued around them, a gentle hush fell over the crowd. The creatures turned their gaze toward Seraphina, who stood at the center of the clearing, her wings shimmering under the light of the lanterns.

"Tonight marks a new beginning for the zoo," she declared. "You have shown great courage and strength in the face of darkness. From this day forth, may the bonds of friendship continue to thrive, and may the magic of this place never fade!"

With those words, the crowd erupted into cheers, their voices echoing through the clearing. The friends looked at one another, knowing that this night was just the beginning of their journey. Together, they had faced incredible challenges, but they had also forged unbreakable bonds.

Chapter 15: The Shadowy Zookeeper

The celebration continued long into the night, the atmosphere filled with laughter, music, and the flickering glow of lanterns that lit up the zoo like a fairytale. Don, Mandy, Timmy, and Jake reveled in the joy of the moment, surrounded by creatures of all shapes and sizes. Yet, as the excitement swirled around them, a lingering sense of unease settled in the pit of their stomachs.

"Can you believe everything we've accomplished?" Jake said, taking a sip of a sparkling drink offered by a nearby fairy. "We faced shadows, solved riddles, and danced like there's no tomorrow!"

Mandy smiled, her eyes reflecting the warmth of the lanterns. "It's incredible! But something feels... off. Like the night isn't quite finished with us yet."

Don furrowed his brow, glancing around at the jubilant crowd. "You think there's more darkness lurking? We defeated Mr. Grimble, didn't we?"

Timmy nodded slowly, feeling the tension in the air. "Yeah, but there's always the possibility that something could rise again. We can't let our guard down."

Just then, the music faded, and the gathering fell silent. The friends exchanged puzzled glances as Seraphina stepped forward, her expression serious.

"Friends, while we celebrate our victory, I must remind you that darkness can linger in unexpected places. The shadows may have been banished, but there are always forces seeking to reclaim what has been lost."

A chill swept through the crowd, and murmurs rippled like waves. Don felt a knot form in his stomach. "What do you mean?"

Seraphina took a deep breath. "There is a figure known as the Shadowy Zookeeper—one who manipulates darkness and seeks to control the magic of this zoo. He has been waiting for the right moment to strike, and I fear he may not be far away."

Just as she spoke, a gust of wind swept through the clearing, extinguishing some of the lanterns and plunging parts of the gathering into shadow. The friends instinctively huddled closer together, their senses heightened.

"Stay together!" Timmy shouted, gripping the hands of his friends.

From the depths of the darkness, a chilling laugh echoed, reverberating around the clearing. The sound was low and menacing, sending shivers down their spines. Suddenly, the shadows coalesced into a figure—tall and cloaked in darkness, with glowing eyes that burned like embers.

"Ah, how delightful!" the figure hissed, a wicked grin spreading across its face. "How brave of you to celebrate while darkness looms nearby. But you have made a grave mistake in believing you could defeat me."

"Who are you?" Don shouted, trying to mask the tremor in his voice. "What do you want?"

"I am the Shadowy Zookeeper, keeper of the darkness that you foolishly tried to dispel!" the figure replied, its voice dripping with malice. "And I have come to reclaim what is rightfully mine. This zoo belongs to the shadows, and I will not let your light extinguish it!"

The creatures around the clearing stirred uneasily, glancing at one another. Don, Mandy, Timmy, and Jake stood firm, their resolve hardening.

"We won't let you take it away!" Jake shouted defiantly. "We've fought too hard to let darkness win!"

The Shadowy Zookeeper laughed, a sound that sent a chill down their spines. "You think your bravery matters? Your light is but a flicker compared to the darkness I command!"

As he spoke, shadows began to swirl around him, forming dark tendrils that stretched out toward the friends. The atmosphere thickened, and the lanterns dimmed further, casting long, eerie shadows across the clearing.

"Protect the light!" Seraphina commanded, stepping forward, her wings shimmering as she called upon the magic of the zoo.

In response, the friends instinctively raised their magical items—the Medallion of the Bat, the seeds from the pumpkin patch, the pearl from the aquarium, and Jake's star-shaped key. Each item glowed brightly, casting a warm light that pushed back against the encroaching darkness.

"Together!" Don shouted, feeling the power of their unity surge through him. "We can face him!"

As they joined their powers, a brilliant beam of light shot forth, illuminating the clearing and cutting through the shadows. The Shadowy Zookeeper snarled, his form twisting in the face of their combined magic.

"You think you can defeat me?" he roared, summoning the shadows to form a barrier around him. "You are nothing!"

But the friends stood resolute, channeling their energies into a concentrated beam. "We are stronger together!" they shouted in unison, their voices echoing with determination.

The light intensified, piercing through the darkness surrounding the Shadowy Zookeeper. He staggered back, struggling against the radiant energy that enveloped him.

"Foolish children!" he spat, rage spilling from his lips. "You cannot defeat me! I am the embodiment of the night!"

As the shadows writhed around him, Timmy took a step forward, gripping the pearl tightly. "You may embody the night, but we embody hope!" he declared. "And hope will always prevail over darkness!"

With that proclamation, the friends poured every ounce of their energy into the light. The beam surged forward, breaking through the shadows and striking the Shadowy Zookeeper directly in the chest.

He howled in fury, the shadows dissipating around him as the light engulfed him. "No! This cannot be!" he screamed, his form unraveling as he was consumed by the brilliance.

As the last remnants of darkness faded, the clearing filled with a warm, golden light. The friends stood together, breathing heavily as they felt the weight of the night lift from their shoulders.

The crowd erupted into cheers, the creatures celebrating the defeat of the Shadowy Zookeeper. "You did it! You drove him away!" a friendly owl hooted, flapping its wings joyfully.

Don, Mandy, Timmy, and Jake exchanged relieved glances, their hearts swelling with pride. "We really did it!" Mandy said, her voice filled with wonder.

Seraphina stepped forward, her expression a mixture of admiration and gratitude. "You have proven that light and hope will always triumph over darkness. Together, you are stronger than any shadow."

The friends basked in the glow of their victory, the warmth of the lanterns flickering around them. They had faced their fears, conquered the darkness, and emerged victorious. But deep down, they knew this was only a chapter in their ongoing journey.

Chapter 16: New Beginnings

As the celebration continued around them, the clearing pulsed with the energy of joy and triumph. Lanterns floated gently above the gathering, their warm glow casting dancing shadows that flickered playfully on the ground. The friends stood together, still buzzing with adrenaline from their recent encounter with the Shadowy Zookeeper.

"Can you believe we actually faced him?" Timmy said, his voice filled with wonder as he looked around at the festivities. "I thought we were done for at one point!"

Mandy chuckled, nudging him playfully. "We almost were! But we held strong together, and that made all the difference."

"I'm just glad we didn't have to fight him alone," Jake added, glancing at the friendly creatures celebrating with them. "This zoo is truly magical."

Just then, Seraphina approached them, her wings shimmering in the lantern light. "I hope you are all well," she said, her voice melodic. "The energy in this place is unlike anything I have ever felt. You have done a great service to the zoo and its inhabitants."

"We couldn't have done it without your help," Don replied, gratitude filling his voice. "Thank you for guiding us through our challenges."

"Your bravery has inspired everyone here," Seraphina continued. "But with the defeat of the Shadowy Zookeeper, it's time for the next phase of your journey. You have proven yourselves to be true protectors of magic."

"What do you mean?" Mandy asked, her brow furrowing with curiosity.

"The magic of this zoo is alive, but it is also fragile," Seraphina explained. "While the shadows have been driven back for now, the balance of magic must be maintained. You each possess unique gifts that can help shape the future of this place."

Jake felt a rush of excitement. "What do we need to do?"

"First, you must unite your magical items—the Medallion of the Bat, the pearl, the seeds, and the star-shaped key," Seraphina instructed. "Together, they will unlock a new source of magic hidden within the zoo. It is a sanctuary that holds the essence of all creatures, a place where magic flows freely."

Don exchanged glances with his friends, feeling the weight of Seraphina's words. "What happens when we unlock this sanctuary?" he asked, a mix of curiosity and apprehension in his voice.

"The sanctuary will become a wellspring of magic, a safe haven for all creatures," Seraphina replied. "But it will also require guardians—those who are willing to protect it from any future threats. That is where you come in."

Mandy nodded, her determination evident. "We're in. We'll do whatever it takes to protect the magic of the zoo."

"Excellent," Seraphina said, her expression softening. "But to unlock the sanctuary, you must journey to the Heart of the Zoo, where the ancient tree stands. That is where the magic resides."

Timmy felt a flutter of excitement and nerves. "How do we get there?"

"Follow the path of light," Seraphina instructed, pointing toward a glowing trail that stretched across the clearing. "It will lead you to the Heart of the Zoo. And remember, the bond you share is your greatest strength."

With that, the friends gathered their magical items, ready for the next leg of their adventure. They stepped onto the path of light, the warmth of the lanterns guiding them forward. The atmosphere crackled with energy as they walked, each step echoing the promise of new beginnings.

The trail wound through the zoo, leading them past familiar sights now imbued with new magic. The once-vibrant colors felt even more vivid, as if the zoo itself was celebrating their journey. They passed by the Haunted Aquarium, where glowing fish swam gracefully in the tanks, and the Enchanted Carousel, now shimmering softly in the moonlight.

As they ventured deeper, they reached a clearing filled with towering trees, their branches stretching high into the sky. In the center stood a magnificent tree, ancient and wise, with roots that seemed to pulse with energy.

"Is this the Heart of the Zoo?" Jake asked, awe evident in his voice.

"It must be!" Mandy replied, stepping closer to the grand tree. The air shimmered around it, and the magical essence felt palpable, like a living heartbeat.

"This is it," Don said, determination etched on his face. "Let's unlock the sanctuary!"

They gathered in a circle around the tree, each friend holding their magical item tightly. "Together, on three!" Timmy said, excitement bubbling within him. "One... two... three!"

As they raised their items high, a blinding light erupted from the tree, enveloping them in a warm glow. The items began to vibrate in unison, resonating with the energy around them.

"Feel the magic!" Mandy shouted, her voice filled with exhilaration.

The light intensified, cascading around them like a waterfall of stars. In that moment, they were connected—hearts, minds, and magic intertwining as one. The essence of the zoo surged through them, empowering each friend with newfound strength.

As the light began to fade, a door formed in the base of the tree, shimmering with ethereal beauty. The door opened slowly, revealing a sanctuary filled with radiant light and vibrant colors. A sense of peace washed over them, and the air hummed with potential.

"Welcome to the Sanctuary of Magic!" a gentle voice echoed from within. It was the spirit of the zoo, a luminous figure that radiated warmth and kindness.

The friends stepped inside, their eyes widening as they took in the breathtaking sights. The sanctuary was alive with magic—creatures of every kind roamed freely, the air filled with laughter and joy.

"Here, you will find the heart of the magic that binds us all," the spirit explained. "But with this gift comes great responsibility. You are now the guardians of this sanctuary. Protect it from any darkness that seeks to disrupt the balance."

Don, Mandy, Timmy, and Jake exchanged glances, feeling the weight of the responsibility but also the excitement that accompanied it. They had come so far, and now they were entrusted with something truly special.

Chapter 17: Guardians of the Sanctuary

The Sanctuary of Magic buzzed with energy, the air alive with enchantment as Don, Mandy, Timmy, and Jake explored their new surroundings. Vibrant colors and playful creatures surrounded them, creating an atmosphere of joy and wonder. The spirit of the zoo floated nearby, illuminating their path with a gentle glow.

"Look at this place!" Jake exclaimed, his eyes wide with amazement as he watched a group of small, fluffy creatures bouncing between the flowers. "It's even more magical than I imagined!"

"It's incredible," Mandy agreed, bending down to pet a creature that looked like a cross between a rabbit and a hummingbird. The tiny creature chirped happily, its wings fluttering in delight.

"The magic here is unlike anything we've ever experienced," Don said, taking in the sights. "But we need to remember our responsibility. We're guardians now."

"Yes," Timmy added, feeling a sense of gravity settle over him. "We must protect this sanctuary and its magic from any darkness that may return."

The spirit of the zoo turned to them, its glowing form radiating warmth. "You are wise beyond your years. Embrace your roles, for the magic of this sanctuary is intertwined with your hearts. Together, you will ensure that it thrives."

As they ventured deeper into the sanctuary, they noticed a clearing filled with shimmering crystals that sparkled like stars. Each crystal pulsed with energy, casting colorful reflections on the surrounding flora.

"What are these?" Don asked, stepping closer to examine one of the crystals.

"They are the Crystals of Connection," the spirit explained. "Each crystal holds the essence of the creatures that inhabit this sanctuary. By connecting with them, you can draw upon their magic and strengthen your bond with the sanctuary."

Mandy reached out, her fingers brushing against the surface of a nearby crystal. Instantly, images flooded her mind—visions of the creatures within the sanctuary, their stories intertwined with the magic of the zoo.

"Wow," she whispered, her eyes wide. "It's like I can feel their emotions. They're all connected!"

"Exactly," the spirit said, its voice soft and soothing. "By understanding the creatures, you'll learn to harness their magic. But with this connection comes responsibility. You must ensure their well-being and protect them from any threats."

Timmy stepped forward, feeling a surge of energy from one of the crystals. "What kind of threats should we be on the lookout for?"

"The shadows may still linger," the spirit warned, its expression growing serious. "Though the Shadowy Zookeeper has been defeated, other forces may seek to disrupt the balance. Darkness can take many forms—fear, doubt, and even those who wish to exploit the magic for their own gain."

Jake felt a shiver run down his spine. "So, we need to be vigilant and prepared for anything."

"Indeed," the spirit replied. "You must also cultivate your abilities and learn to work together as guardians. The magic of the sanctuary will respond to your unity and trust in one another."

With a sense of purpose, the friends decided to train and bond with the creatures within the sanctuary. They spent the next few days learning about the various animals and their unique magical properties, forming connections that would strengthen their abilities.

One morning, they gathered in the clearing, ready to begin their training. "What should we focus on first?" Don asked, glancing at the spirit for guidance.

"Begin with the basics," the spirit advised. "Focus on understanding your magical items and how they interact with the sanctuary. You can start by connecting with the Crystals of Connection."

The friends nodded, each approaching a crystal that resonated with them. As they placed their hands on the cool surfaces, they felt a wave of energy wash over them, connecting them to the magic of the sanctuary.

Mandy closed her eyes and concentrated. Visions flooded her mind—images of playful creatures dancing through fields of flowers, the soft rustle of leaves, and the gentle murmur of a flowing stream. She felt a deep sense of peace and happiness, the magic of nature coursing through her veins.

"I can feel the connection," she said, her voice filled with awe. "It's beautiful!"

Timmy focused on a crystal that pulsed with a deep blue light. As he connected, he felt the power of water surging within him, the calming presence of the ocean flowing through his senses. "It's like I'm swimming in the sea!" he exclaimed, his excitement palpable.

Jake placed his hand on a vibrant green crystal, feeling the energy of the earth beneath him. Images of plants growing, creatures burrowing into the soil, and the rhythm of nature's heartbeat filled his mind. "This is incredible," he said, feeling a sense of grounding and stability.

Don approached a crystal that radiated golden light, representing the essence of light and courage. As he connected, he felt a surge of bravery course through him, empowering him with confidence. "I can feel the light within me," he declared, his heart swelling with purpose.

After spending time connecting with the crystals, the friends gathered together, their energies intertwined. "This is just the beginning," Don said, determination shining in his eyes. "We're becoming stronger, and we can protect this place!"

"But we need to be cautious," Mandy added, a hint of worry creeping into her voice. "If the darkness can return, we have to be prepared for anything."

"Let's continue our training," Timmy suggested. "We should practice using our magic together."

As the days turned into weeks, the friends dedicated themselves to honing their skills. They trained under the guidance of Seraphina and other creatures in the sanctuary, learning to channel their powers and work together as a united front.

One afternoon, as they practiced harnessing their abilities, the air grew heavy with anticipation. They could sense a change in the atmosphere, a ripple of energy that hinted at something looming.

"What's happening?" Jake asked, glancing around, his heart racing.

Seraphina appeared, her expression serious. "Guardians, there is a disturbance in the sanctuary. Shadows are beginning to creep back into our world. We must be prepared to face whatever is coming."

Mandy felt a chill run down her spine. "What do we need to do?"

"Stand united and trust in your magic," Seraphina instructed. "The darkness may test you, but if you work together, you can protect the sanctuary and all its creatures."

With renewed determination, the friends stood tall, their magical items glowing brightly at their sides. They knew they had faced darkness before, and they would do so again—together.

Chapter 18: The Return of Shadows

The atmosphere in the Sanctuary of Magic thickened with tension as the shadows began to creep back, swirling ominously at the edges of the clearing. Don, Mandy, Timmy, and Jake stood together, their hearts racing, sensing that the time had come to face a new threat.

"Stay close," Don said, gripping the Medallion of the Bat tightly. The familiar warmth pulsed in his palm, reassuring him. "We've trained for this. We can handle whatever comes our way."

Mandy nodded, holding the glowing seeds in her hands. "We've faced darkness before, and we can do it again. We just have to believe in each other and the magic we've created."

As the friends stood united, the shadows grew bolder, coiling around the trees and creeping toward the heart of the sanctuary. The vibrant colors of the flowers began to fade, dimmed by the encroaching darkness.

"Look!" Timmy pointed toward the edge of the clearing. From the depths of the shadows, figures began to emerge—dark, twisted versions of the creatures that once filled the sanctuary with life and joy. Their eyes glowed with malevolence, and their forms flickered like wisps of smoke.

"Those were once the guardians of the sanctuary," the spirit of the zoo said, its voice tinged with sadness. "They have been corrupted by the Shadowy Zookeeper's magic. We must free them before it's too late."

Jake took a deep breath, adrenaline pumping through him. "How do we do that?"

"By confronting their fears and showing them the light they've forgotten," the spirit replied. "You have the power to break the darkness that binds them."

The friends exchanged determined glances. "We can do this together," Don said, his voice steady. "Let's not let them fall to the shadows."

With a shared sense of purpose, they stepped forward, facing the dark creatures. "You're not alone!" Mandy called out, her voice strong. "We're here to help you remember who you are!"

The corrupted creatures paused, their glowing eyes flickering as if unsure. For a moment, the shadows around them wavered, revealing glimpses of their former selves—creatures of light and magic.

"Come back to us!" Timmy shouted, feeling the power of the water stone surge within him. "You don't have to stay in the darkness!"

The lead creature—a once-gentle fox with glimmering fur—took a hesitant step forward, its eyes reflecting a flicker of recognition. "We... we are lost," it said, its voice trembling. "The shadows have taken hold, and we cannot break free."

"We'll help you!" Jake called out, holding up the star-shaped key. "Together, we can overcome the darkness!"

As they spoke, the shadows began to swirl around the corrupted creatures, threatening to consume them again. The friends quickly gathered, forming a protective circle.

"Let's channel our magic!" Don shouted. "On three!"

The friends nodded, gripping their magical items tightly. "One... two... three!"

They raised their items high, unleashing a beam of light that surged toward the creatures. The energy pulsed, creating a wave of warmth that washed over the corrupted fox and its companions.

"Feel the light!" Mandy urged, focusing on the warmth radiating from the seeds. "You are not lost! Remember the magic within you!"

As the light enveloped the creatures, their forms began to shift and shimmer, breaking through the darkness that bound them. The shadows recoiled, hissing in frustration, but the friends stood firm, channeling their energy into the beam.

The lead fox shook its head, its eyes clearing as it began to remember. "We were guardians! We protected the magic of the sanctuary!"

"Yes!" Jake shouted, feeling the energy of the key surge through him. "You are still guardians! You can fight against the shadows!"

With that, the fox stepped forward, joining the friends in the circle of light. The other corrupted creatures followed, their eyes brightening as they felt the warmth of the magic rekindling within them.

As the last remnants of darkness began to dissolve, the clearing erupted in a blinding flash of light. The shadows shrieked, retreating into the depths of the sanctuary, unable to withstand the power of unity and hope.

When the light faded, the friends looked around, breathless. The creatures that had once been corrupted stood beside them, their forms restored to their vibrant, magical selves.

"Thank you!" the fox exclaimed, its voice filled with gratitude. "We were lost in the darkness, but your light has guided us home!"

The friends exchanged relieved glances, their hearts swelling with joy. "We couldn't have done it without you!" Don replied, feeling a sense of triumph.

But before they could celebrate, the air shifted once more. The shadows stirred at the edges of the clearing, coiling like smoke.

"Don't let your guard down!" the spirit warned, its voice urgent. "The darkness will seek to retaliate!"

Just as it spoke, a powerful gust of wind swept through the clearing, followed by a chilling laugh that echoed ominously. The Shadowy Zookeeper re-emerged, his form shrouded in darkness, his glowing eyes filled with fury.

"You think you've won?" he hissed, his voice dripping with malice. "You may have restored the guardians, but you will never banish me!"

The friends stood tall, their resolve unwavering. "We won't let you take this sanctuary!" Mandy shouted, her voice fierce. "We're ready to fight!"

"Very well," the Shadowy Zookeeper sneered. "Let's see how strong your little light truly is!"

With that, he unleashed a wave of shadows that surged toward them, threatening to consume everything in its path. The friends braced themselves, channeling their energy and the magic of the restored guardians.

"Together!" Don shouted, raising the Medallion of the Bat high. "We can face this!"

As the shadows collided with their magic, a dazzling light erupted from their united forces, pushing back against the encroaching darkness. The clearing shimmered with energy, the colors brightening as the friends focused their powers.

The restored guardians joined them, adding their magic to the mix. The vibrant energy surged, forming a protective barrier that pushed against the shadows.

"You will not win!" Timmy declared, feeling the power of the water surge within him. "The light will always prevail!"

The Shadowy Zookeeper howled in fury, his form writhing as he struggled against the radiant energy. "No! I will not be defeated by mere children!"

With one final surge of determination, the friends directed their magic toward the Zookeeper. The light intensified, breaking through the darkness and illuminating the clearing in a brilliant display of colors.

"Feel the light!" Jake shouted, pouring every ounce of strength into their combined magic. "You are nothing without the shadows!"

With a deafening roar, the shadows shattered, and the Shadowy Zookeeper was engulfed in a blinding light. As the darkness dissolved around him, he let out a final scream, and then he was gone.

The clearing fell silent, the echoes of battle fading away. The friends stood together, breathing heavily, their hearts racing as they processed what had just happened.

Chapter 19: Uncharted Waters

The glow of the Sanctuary of Magic enveloped Don, Mandy, Timmy, and Jake as they stood together, basking in the triumph of their recent victory over the Shadowy Zookeeper. The air was filled with the scent of blooming flowers and the gentle hum of magic pulsating through the clearing. Though the immediate threat had been vanquished, a new chapter awaited them—one filled with opportunities to deepen their connection to the sanctuary and its magical inhabitants.

"Now that we've established ourselves as guardians, what do we do next?" Jake asked, glancing around at the vibrant surroundings. Creatures of all shapes and sizes were exploring their newfound freedom, their laughter ringing out like music in the air.

Seraphina floated nearby, her wings shimmering under the soft light of the lanterns. "Your journey is just beginning," she replied, her voice warm and inviting. "There is much to learn about your roles as guardians, and you must explore the depths of the magic that resides within this sanctuary."

Mandy felt a flutter of excitement in her stomach. "What do you mean by 'the depths of the magic'?"

"The magic of the sanctuary is connected to every creature, plant, and element within it," Seraphina explained. "To become true guardians, you must learn to navigate this magic and understand its many forms. This includes exploring the enchanted waters of the sanctuary."

"The waters?" Timmy echoed, intrigued. "What's special about them?"

"The enchanted waters hold the essence of life and magic," Seraphina said. "They connect the sanctuary to the broader magic of the zoo. By diving into these waters, you can gain insights into your powers and learn to harness them."

Don's eyes sparkled with curiosity. "How do we get there?"

"Follow the path of the shimmering river," Seraphina instructed, pointing toward a narrow stream that wound its way through the sanctuary. "It will lead you to the Enchanted Waters."

Excited chatter filled the air as the friends set off, their footsteps light with anticipation. The path along the river was lined with vibrant flowers, their petals opening and closing as if they were nodding in encouragement. The soothing sound of flowing water accompanied them, creating a serene atmosphere.

As they walked, Jake glanced at the reflections in the water. "It's almost hypnotizing," he remarked, watching the way the light danced across the surface. "I can't wait to see what's in there!"

Mandy smiled, taking in the beauty around her. "I wonder if we'll discover anything new about our magic. Each trial has shown us different aspects of ourselves."

Soon, they reached a larger clearing where the stream widened into a serene pool. The water sparkled like diamonds, and the atmosphere felt charged with energy. "This must be it," Timmy said, his voice filled with awe.

As they approached the edge of the pool, a gentle mist rose from the water, wrapping around them like a warm embrace. The spirit of the sanctuary appeared beside them, its luminous form radiating warmth. "Welcome to the Enchanted Waters," it said, its voice soothing. "Here, you will connect with the magic that flows through the zoo and discover your true potential."

"Is there anything we need to do?" Don asked, feeling a mix of excitement and nervousness.

"Simply immerse yourselves in the waters and open your hearts to the magic within," the spirit instructed. "Let the waters guide you on your journey."

Without hesitation, the friends stepped forward, wading into the cool water. As they submerged themselves, a wave of energy surged through them, wrapping around their bodies like a gentle current. The sensation was invigorating, awakening every fiber of their being.

"Wow, this feels amazing!" Jake exclaimed, feeling the magic swirl around him. "I can almost see the colors dancing!"

Mandy closed her eyes, allowing the water to envelop her. Images began to form in her mind—visions of creatures she had connected with, the light of the sanctuary shining brightly in her heart. She could feel the energy of the sanctuary coursing through her, intertwining with her very essence.

Timmy gasped, his eyes widening as he felt the water connecting him to the vast ocean beyond the zoo. "It's like I'm swimming in the waves! I can feel the pull of the tides!"

As the friends swam deeper into the pool, they began to feel the magic manifesting around them. Glowing fish swam gracefully past, leaving trails of shimmering light in their wake. The water felt alive, responding to their presence with warmth and encouragement.

"Focus on your magic!" Seraphina called from the edge of the pool, her voice echoing in the tranquil air. "Let the waters reveal your true potential!"

Don took a deep breath, centering himself as he concentrated on the energy surrounding him. He could feel the warmth of the Medallion of the Bat resonating with the waters, merging their magic. Images of the battles they had fought and the friendships they had forged filled his mind.

Suddenly, a brilliant flash erupted from the water, and a shimmering light enveloped Don. He felt a surge of energy coursing through him, a connection to the night and the creatures that roamed within it.

"I can feel the night sky!" he shouted, exhilaration filling his voice. "I'm connected to the stars!"

Mandy, feeling the magic flow through her, began to rise above the water, her body surrounded by a halo of light. "The magic of the flowers! It's blossoming within me!" she exclaimed, her laughter ringing out like chimes.

Timmy swam closer to the edge of the pool, feeling the water calling to him. As he concentrated, he felt the essence of the ocean surge within him. "I'm one with the currents!" he shouted joyfully, his spirit soaring.

Jake, too, began to feel the connection strengthen. The star-shaped key pulsed with energy, guiding him to explore his abilities. "I can see everything!" he cried out, feeling the magic illuminating his path. "It's like I'm flying!"

As they embraced their powers, the waters began to shimmer and swirl around them, forming intricate patterns that danced in the air. The friends felt the magic binding them together, a reminder of their shared journey and the strength of their bond.

"Together, we are unstoppable!" Don declared, his voice filled with determination.

Just then, a ripple broke the surface of the water, and a powerful force surged from the depths. The friends felt a sudden shift in energy, and the once-warm waters turned icy cold.

"What's happening?" Timmy shouted, panic rising in his chest.

The spirit of the sanctuary appeared, its expression turning grave. "Something is stirring in the depths," it warned. "The shadows may have retreated, but they will not remain silent for long."

As the waters roiled, dark shapes began to emerge from the depths—twisted, shadowy figures that reached toward the surface, seeking to pull the friends down into the darkness.

"We have to fight it!" Jake shouted, rallying his friends. "Channel your magic!"

With their hearts pounding, they concentrated, drawing upon the strength of the sanctuary. The waters responded to their call, and beams of light erupted from each of their magical items, intertwining to create a protective barrier.

"Stay together!" Mandy shouted, her voice steady. "We can push them back!"

As they fought against the encroaching shadows, the friends felt their bond strengthening. The light pulsed brighter, illuminating the darkness and pushing the twisted forms away from the edge of the pool.

"We won't let you take this sanctuary!" Don shouted, channeling every ounce of courage into their magic.

With a final surge of energy, they directed their combined magic toward the shadows, breaking through the darkness with a brilliant flash of light. The shadows recoiled, screeching in fury as they were consumed by the radiant energy.

The waters settled, the once-icy tendrils dissipating into nothingness. The friends stood together, panting but triumphant, their magic still glowing around them.

Chapter 20: A Call to Adventure

The atmosphere in the Sanctuary of Magic settled into a serene calm after the battle against the shadows. The friends stood at the edge of the shimmering pool, reflecting on their experiences and what lay ahead. Each challenge they faced had brought them closer together, and the sense of unity radiated from them like the light of the lanterns that filled the sanctuary.

"I can't believe how quickly everything escalated," Jake said, shaking his head as he dried off with a warm breeze that swirled around them. "One moment we're celebrating, and the next, we're fighting off shadows!"

"It's a reminder that we need to stay vigilant," Don replied, glancing at the shimmering pool. "But we also have to enjoy the magic we're protecting. We've accomplished so much, and we deserve to celebrate our victories too!"

Mandy smiled, feeling the warmth of the sun filtering through the leaves above them. "Maybe we should host a festival! A way to celebrate our new roles and bring everyone together."

Timmy's eyes lit up at the idea. "That sounds amazing! We could invite all the creatures from the zoo and showcase the magic of the sanctuary."

Seraphina floated closer, her wings shimmering. "A festival is a wonderful idea! It would strengthen the bonds between the guardians and the inhabitants of the sanctuary. It's essential for everyone to know that they are safe and that magic is alive."

"We could include games, performances, and magical exhibitions!" Jake added, already imagining the possibilities. "There could be storytelling, dancing, and even contests to showcase our powers!"

"Let's do it!" Don exclaimed, enthusiasm bubbling in his chest. "We can organize everything together, and it'll be a great way to bond with the creatures and celebrate what we've achieved."

With newfound excitement, the friends set off to plan the festival. They began by exploring the sanctuary, gathering ideas and brainstorming activities that would celebrate their unity and the magic of the zoo.

As they moved through the lush landscapes, they stumbled upon a group of friendly creatures—bunnies with wings, glowing butterflies, and even a few small dragons flitting about. The sight filled them with joy, and they stopped to speak with the creatures.

"Hello, little friends!" Mandy called, waving at the gathering. "We're planning a festival, and we'd love for you to join us!"

The bunnies perked up, their ears twitching with interest. "A festival? That sounds wonderful!" one of them exclaimed, hopping closer. "What will it be like?"

"It will be a celebration of magic and friendship!" Timmy explained, his excitement infectious. "We'll have games, performances, and even a place for everyone to showcase their talents!"

The creatures exchanged excited glances, their eyes shining with anticipation. "We would love to help!" a small dragon chimed in, its scales glinting in the light. "We can put on a fire dance!"

"Count us in!" the butterflies fluttered, their wings sparkling like gemstones. "We can create beautiful displays in the air!"

With the help of the magical creatures, the friends quickly began organizing the festival. They mapped out the sanctuary, designating areas for games, performances, and food stalls. Laughter and excitement filled the air as they collaborated with the inhabitants, each creature eager to contribute their talents.

Days passed, and the festival preparations took shape. Colorful decorations adorned the trees, and pathways were lined with shimmering lights. The air buzzed with anticipation as creatures from all corners of the sanctuary arrived to participate.

As the sun dipped below the horizon on the day of the festival, the sanctuary transformed into a breathtaking wonderland. Lanterns glowed warmly, casting a magical light over the clearing. The scent of delicious treats wafted through the air, drawing everyone together.

"Are you ready?" Jake asked, his voice tinged with excitement.

"Absolutely!" Mandy replied, her eyes sparkling. "This is going to be incredible!"

As the festivities kicked off, creatures began to gather, their laughter echoing through the sanctuary. Games filled the clearing, from magical ring tosses to obstacle courses designed for both small and large creatures.

Timmy led a group of friends in a storytelling circle, where they shared tales of their adventures, weaving magic and friendship into each story. "And that's when we faced the shadows together!" he concluded, eliciting cheers and applause from the gathered crowd.

Meanwhile, Jake organized a magical dance competition. Creatures twirled and leaped, showcasing their unique abilities in a dazzling display. The small dragons performed a mesmerizing fire dance, filling the air with sparkling embers that twinkled like stars.

As the sun set, Seraphina gathered everyone around the center of the clearing. "Thank you all for joining us tonight," she said, her voice resonating with warmth. "This festival is a celebration of our unity, the strength we've found in each other, and the magic that binds us all. Let us remember that together, we can overcome any darkness!"

The crowd erupted into cheers, and the friends exchanged proud smiles. They had created a gathering that highlighted the spirit of the sanctuary, and their bond had only grown stronger.

Just as the festivities reached a crescendo, a sudden chill swept through the air. The laughter and excitement dimmed, and a shadow fell over the clearing. The friends exchanged worried glances, feeling the energy shift.

"Do you feel that?" Don asked, his brow furrowing. "Something isn't right."

Before they could react, a dark figure emerged from the trees, cloaked in shadows. It was a tall, menacing figure, its glowing eyes piercing through the darkness. The laughter of the festival faded, replaced by an uneasy silence.

"Did you really think you could celebrate while I remain?" the figure snarled, its voice a low rumble. "I am the Night Warden, and I will reclaim what belongs to the shadows!"

"Not again!" Mandy shouted, stepping forward. "We defeated the Shadowy Zookeeper, and we won't let you take our sanctuary!"

The Night Warden let out a chilling laugh, the shadows swirling around him. "You are naive, children. The darkness is ever-present, and you cannot escape its grasp!"

With a swift motion, the Night Warden unleashed a wave of shadows, engulfing the festival area in darkness. Creatures scattered, their joyful energy dissipating as panic set in.

"Stand together!" Don shouted, rallying his friends. "We've faced darkness before, and we can do it again!"

The friends gripped their magical items tightly, channeling their powers. "Focus on the light!" Timmy called out, feeling the energy of the sanctuary pulsing around them.

As they raised their items high, the sanctuary responded, illuminating the area with a brilliant light. The shadows recoiled, but the Night Warden pressed forward, determined to reclaim his power.

"You think your light can defeat me?" he bellowed, fury boiling in his voice. "I thrive in darkness!"

But the friends stood firm, their resolve unwavering. "We won't back down!" Mandy shouted, her voice fierce. "We are guardians, and we will protect this sanctuary!"

With that declaration, they unleashed their magic, a concentrated beam of light that surged toward the Night Warden. The darkness writhed and twisted around him, but the power of their unity cut through it like a blade.

"Feel the light!" Don shouted, pouring every ounce of energy into their combined magic. "You will not take this sanctuary from us!"

The beam struck the Night Warden, illuminating the clearing with a radiant glow. He howled in rage, shadows swirling around him as he struggled against the light. "No! This cannot be!"

But the friends pressed on, their spirits united. The energy surged through them, creating a barrier of light that enveloped the Night Warden, forcing the shadows to retreat.

As the light grew brighter, the darkness shattered, and with a final, deafening roar, the Night Warden dissolved into nothingness.

The clearing fell silent, the air still buzzing with energy as the shadows receded. The friends looked at one another, breathless from the confrontation.

Chapter 21: The Depths of the Sanctuary

The aftermath of the Night Warden's defeat left a palpable sense of urgency in the Sanctuary of Magic. Though the festival resumed with laughter and joy, the friends understood that the threat of darkness would always loom over them. As guardians, they had to delve deeper into their powers and the mysteries of the sanctuary.

"We need to understand more about what we're up against," Don said, gathering the group beneath the ancient tree, which stood tall and proud at the heart of the sanctuary. The tree's trunk glowed softly, illuminating their faces as they prepared for their next steps.

Mandy nodded, a thoughtful look on her face. "Maybe there are hidden areas within the sanctuary that we haven't explored yet. We should find out more about the magic that resides here."

Timmy glanced toward the shimmering pool where they had first discovered the Enchanted Waters. "And what about the depths of the sanctuary? The spirit mentioned there were layers of magic waiting to be uncovered."

"That's a great idea!" Jake replied, his eyes sparkling with excitement. "We should explore everything this sanctuary has to offer. Maybe there are clues that can help us defend against the darkness."

With their purpose set, the friends decided to venture toward the deeper areas of the sanctuary. They knew that the magic surrounding them was vast, and understanding it fully would be key to their roles as guardians.

As they journeyed, the landscape began to change. The vibrant colors of the flowers and trees gave way to more muted tones, with towering cliffs and rocky formations rising around them. The air felt charged with energy, and the whispers of magic echoed through the shadows.

"Stay close together," Don instructed as they walked. "We don't know what might be lurking in the depths."

As they continued down the path, they reached a massive cave entrance, shrouded in mist. The cool air wafted out, filled with the scent of earth and mystery. "This must be it," Mandy said, her voice a mix of excitement and apprehension. "The entrance to the deeper parts of the sanctuary."

Timmy stepped forward, peering into the dark cave. "Should we go in?"

"Absolutely," Jake replied, determination lighting up his face. "We're guardians now. We need to uncover the secrets within."

Taking a deep breath, they entered the cave, the sound of their footsteps echoing off the walls. As they moved further inside, the darkness enveloped them, but the glow from their magical items illuminated the path ahead.

"Can you feel that?" Timmy whispered, sensing a strong current of magic flowing through the air. "It's like the cave is alive."

"Yes," Seraphina's voice echoed softly beside them, guiding their steps. "The magic within these walls is ancient and powerful. It connects to the very essence of the sanctuary."

As they ventured deeper, they found themselves in a large cavern filled with sparkling crystals that reflected their light, creating a dazzling display of colors. "Wow!" Mandy exclaimed, her eyes wide with wonder. "This place is breathtaking!"

The crystals pulsed rhythmically, as if responding to their presence. "These are the Crystals of Harmony," Seraphina explained. "They hold the memories and magic of the sanctuary, preserving its history and secrets."

"Can we connect with them?" Don asked, intrigued by the shimmering display.

"Yes, but be prepared," Seraphina warned. "Connecting with the Crystals of Harmony may reveal hidden truths and ancient wisdom, but it could also uncover fears you must confront."

With a nod of determination, the friends stepped closer to the largest crystal at the center of the cavern. Its surface glimmered with colors that seemed to dance with life. "Let's do this together," Jake said, reaching out to place his hand on the crystal. The others followed suit, forming a circle around it.

As their hands made contact with the crystal, a wave of energy surged through them. Their surroundings dissolved into a swirl of colors, and they were plunged into a vision—images and memories flooding their minds.

They found themselves standing in a lush landscape, filled with vibrant creatures and magical beings. They witnessed scenes from the past: guardians protecting the sanctuary, celebrating victories over darkness, and forging unbreakable bonds with the creatures of the zoo.

"This is incredible!" Mandy exclaimed, her voice filled with awe. "It's like we're reliving their memories."

But then the images shifted, and they saw a darker scene—shadows creeping in, consuming the joy and light, leaving only despair in their wake. The guardians fought valiantly, but one by one, they fell to the shadows.

"No! They're losing!" Timmy shouted, feeling a pang of fear grip his heart.

"Focus!" Don urged, feeling the weight of the vision. "We can't let that happen again!"

As the darkness closed in on the guardians, the friends felt a surge of determination. "We're here now!" Jake shouted, his voice ringing clear. "We can change this!"

In that moment of unity, the crystal pulsed with energy, and a wave of light erupted from the friends, pushing back against the shadows. The darkness began to dissolve, and the vision transformed into a radiant display of hope and resilience.

"Together!" Mandy shouted, channeling their combined magic into the crystal. "We can break the cycle!"

With every ounce of energy, they pushed against the shadows, their magic illuminating the cavern. The darkness receded, and the image of the past guardians grew stronger, their spirits reignited by the light.

As the shadows faded, the vision shifted once more, revealing the sanctuary in its current glory—filled with laughter, color, and vibrant life. The friends stood together, witnessing the impact of their actions.

When the vision finally faded, they found themselves back in the cavern, breathless and filled with emotion. "What just happened?" Timmy asked, his voice shaking slightly.

"The Crystals of Harmony have shown you the past," Seraphina explained, her voice gentle. "They revealed the struggles of previous guardians, but also the strength that comes from unity and hope."

"We saw the darkness they faced," Don said, feeling a sense of responsibility wash over him. "But we also saw how important it is to stand together."

"Exactly," Seraphina affirmed. "You are the new guardians of the sanctuary, and you have the power to shape its future. The darkness will always seek to return, but as long as you stand united, you can protect what is precious."

Mandy nodded, a determined spark igniting in her eyes. "We won't let the shadows win. We'll learn from the past and ensure the sanctuary thrives."

With a renewed sense of purpose, the friends began to explore the cavern further. They uncovered hidden chambers filled with more crystals, each one unique and resonating with different aspects of magic. They spent hours connecting with the crystals, learning about the history of the sanctuary and the roles of the guardians who had come before them.

As they delved deeper into the depths, they felt a greater connection to the sanctuary and its magic. They discovered that the Crystals of Harmony not only held memories but also served as conduits for their powers. The more they learned, the more their abilities grew.

But as the day turned into evening, a new realization dawned upon them. "We should get back to the festival," Jake said, glancing at the time. "I'm sure everyone is waiting for us."

"Right," Timmy agreed, feeling a sense of urgency. "We need to share what we've learned and reinforce the bonds between us."

As they made their way back through the cave, the friends felt a sense of excitement building within them. They had discovered the depths of the sanctuary and uncovered the legacy of the guardians. Now, they were ready to embrace their roles and protect the magic that flowed through their world.

When they finally emerged from the cave, the night sky sparkled with stars, and the festival had continued in their absence. Creatures danced and laughed, the atmosphere alive with joy.

"Welcome back!" a voice called, and they turned to see Seraphina floating toward them, her expression beaming with pride. "Did you find what you were looking for?"

"Yes!" Mandy exclaimed, her eyes shining. "We learned so much about the sanctuary and the past guardians. It was incredible!"

"Then let's celebrate our newfound knowledge!" Seraphina said, her voice filled with joy. "Your journey as guardians has only just begun, and tonight, we will honor it."

With that, the friends rejoined the festivities, sharing their experiences and the magic they had discovered. As they danced and laughed, they felt the bond of friendship grow stronger, intertwined with the magic of the sanctuary.

Together, they were ready to embrace their roles, prepared to face whatever challenges awaited them. The darkness may always loom, but the light of their friendship would shine brighter, guiding them through any storm.

Chapter 22: The Whispering Woods

The festival that followed their deep exploration of the Sanctuary of Magic was a vibrant celebration of unity and resilience. The friends reveled in the joy of the moment, surrounded by creatures they had grown to love, each one contributing to the festivities in unique ways. Lanterns twinkled above, casting a warm glow, while the sounds of laughter and music filled the air, creating a magical atmosphere.

As the night wore on, Don, Mandy, Timmy, and Jake gathered around a cozy bonfire, the flames dancing in the cool night air. They reflected on their journey, discussing the lessons they had learned and the responsibilities they now bore as guardians.

"Can you believe how far we've come?" Mandy said, her eyes sparkling with excitement. "It feels like just yesterday we were wandering through the zoo, completely unaware of the magic that existed here."

"I know!" Timmy replied, a grin spreading across his face. "We've faced so many challenges together. It's amazing to think we're now protectors of this sanctuary."

Jake nodded, a thoughtful expression on his face. "But we have to remain vigilant. The Night Warden was just one of many shadows that could threaten us. We can't let our guard down."

Don leaned forward, gazing into the fire. "What do you think our next challenge will be? With everything we've learned, I feel like we're only just beginning to scratch the surface of our powers."

Just then, Seraphina approached, her wings shimmering softly in the firelight. "Your instincts are sharp, young guardians," she said, her voice melodious. "There are always new adventures waiting for those willing to explore."

"What do you mean?" Jake asked, curious.

"Beyond the sanctuary lies the Whispering Woods," Seraphina explained. "It is a realm filled with magic and mystery, but also with challenges that will test your abilities as guardians."

"What kind of challenges?" Mandy asked, her heart racing with a mix of excitement and apprehension.

"The woods are home to ancient spirits and magical beings," Seraphina continued. "They may help you, but they can also deceive you. You must navigate the woods with care and trust your instincts."

Timmy's eyes widened. "That sounds incredible! We should explore the Whispering Woods!"

"I agree," Don said, feeling a surge of adventure. "We've faced darkness before, and we're ready to face whatever lies ahead."

Seraphina smiled, her expression filled with encouragement. "Then I suggest you prepare for your journey. The woods are vast, and it's best to go in with a plan. The magic you've cultivated will guide you, but listen closely to the whispers around you."

With their destination set, the friends spent the next morning preparing for their journey. They gathered supplies, including snacks, magical items, and anything else they thought might be useful. Excitement buzzed in the air as they made their way toward the edge of the sanctuary, where the Whispering Woods began.

As they approached the entrance, the trees loomed tall and ancient, their branches swaying gently as if welcoming them. A sense of mystery hung in the air, and the sound of leaves rustling echoed like whispers.

"Here we go," Jake said, glancing at his friends. "Stay close together, and remember to listen to the whispers."

With that, they stepped into the woods, the atmosphere changing as the sunlight filtered through the leaves, casting dappled shadows on the forest floor. The air was thick with the scent of damp earth and the sweet aroma of blooming flowers.

As they ventured deeper, the whispers grew louder, swirling around them like a gentle breeze. "What do you think they're saying?" Timmy asked, straining to listen.

"I can't quite make it out," Mandy replied, her brow furrowed in concentration. "But it feels like they're calling to us, guiding us."

Don took a deep breath, feeling the energy of the woods pulse around him. "Let's keep moving. The magic here is alive, and I can feel it pulling us forward."

They continued along the winding path, following the sound of the whispers. The trees began to shift, forming archways that opened up to breathtaking clearings filled with vibrant flowers and glowing creatures.

Suddenly, they stumbled upon a glade where the sunlight poured in, illuminating a majestic tree with shimmering leaves. A small pond lay at its base, and the water sparkled like diamonds.

"Look at that!" Jake exclaimed, pointing toward the tree. "It's beautiful!"

As they approached, they noticed tiny lights flickering around the tree—fireflies dancing in a mesmerizing display. The whispers grew louder, swirling around them like a song.

"It's enchanting," Mandy breathed, feeling drawn to the tree. "I can feel the magic flowing through this place."

Suddenly, a soft voice broke through the whispers. "Welcome, travelers. You have entered the Heart of the Whispering Woods."

The friends turned to see a small, ethereal figure floating above the pond. It was a fairy, her wings shimmering in the light like stained glass. Her eyes sparkled with kindness and wisdom.

"We are the keepers of the woods, and we have watched your journey," the fairy continued. "Your bravery and unity have brought you here. But beware, for the woods hold both beauty and danger."

"What kind of danger?" Don asked, feeling a sense of unease.

"Many seek the power of the woods for their own gain," the fairy explained. "The shadows linger, waiting for an opportunity to seize control. You must remain vigilant and prove your worth to earn the trust of the spirits."

"How do we do that?" Mandy inquired, her determination shining through.

"By facing the trials of the woods," the fairy replied. "Each trial will test your courage, wisdom, and unity. Only by overcoming them will you earn the spirits' blessing."

The friends exchanged glances, a mix of excitement and apprehension settling over them. "We're ready to face whatever challenges come our way," Timmy declared, his voice steady.

"Very well," the fairy said, her wings fluttering gently. "Your first trial begins now. Follow the path of the glowing stones and listen closely to the whispers. They will guide you."

With that, the fairy gestured toward a path lined with glowing stones that illuminated the way ahead. The friends took a deep breath and set off, ready to face their first challenge in the Whispering Woods.

As they walked, the whispers swirled around them, revealing snippets of advice and warnings. "Trust your instincts," they urged. "Listen to the heart of the woods."

The path wound through dense trees, and the light began to fade as the sun dipped lower in the sky. The air grew cooler, and an eerie stillness settled over the woods. Shadows danced at the corners of their vision, but the friends pressed on, their determination unwavering.

Suddenly, the ground beneath them trembled, and a low rumble echoed through the air. The friends exchanged worried glances, but before they could react, the ground split open, revealing a dark chasm.

"Whoa!" Jake exclaimed, stepping back in surprise. "What is happening?"

"Don't let fear take hold!" Don shouted, trying to rally their spirits. "We can't turn back now!"

Just then, a figure emerged from the shadows of the chasm—tall and cloaked in darkness, it loomed over them with glowing eyes. The air grew heavy with tension as the creature stepped forward, its voice echoing like thunder.

"Only those who possess true courage may pass," it growled. "Face your fears, or be consumed by the shadows!"

"What do we do?" Timmy asked, his heart racing. "We can't let it intimidate us!"

"Stay together!" Mandy urged, feeling a surge of determination. "We've faced darkness before, and we can do it again!"

As the creature advanced, the friends held hands, forming a united front. "We are guardians of the magic!" Jake shouted, channeling their strength. "We won't let you stop us!"

With that declaration, they focused on their magical items, channeling their energy into a radiant light that pushed back against the creature's darkness. The glowing stones beneath their feet pulsed with energy, amplifying their magic.

"Feel the light!" Don cried, his voice filled with conviction. "We will not be afraid!"

As the light surged forth, the creature let out a roar, its form writhing in the brightness. "No! You cannot defy me!"

But the friends stood firm, their hearts united in their determination. The shadows began to retreat, the creature's power waning against the force of their magic.

With one final push, they directed their energy toward the creature, illuminating the darkness and breaking through the shadows that sought to consume them.

As the light enveloped the creature, it let out a final cry before dissolving into the air. The ground stopped trembling, and the shadows receded, revealing the glowing path ahead.

Chapter 23: The Trial of Echoes

After facing the dark creature in the Whispering Woods, Don, Mandy, Timmy, and Jake felt a surge of confidence coursing through them. They had proven their courage and unity, but they knew there were more challenges ahead. The whispers of the woods beckoned them forward, leading them deeper into the heart of the sanctuary.

As they continued along the path, the trees began to thicken, their branches intertwining above to form a natural canopy. Sunlight filtered through the leaves, creating a mesmerizing play of light and shadow on the forest floor. The atmosphere felt charged, as if the very air were alive with magic.

"What's next?" Timmy asked, glancing around. "We faced the darkness. Are there more trials?"

Seraphina appeared beside them, her wings shimmering in the dappled light. "Yes, brave guardians. The next trial you will face is known as the Trial of Echoes. It will test not only your courage but also your ability to listen and trust in your instincts."

"What does that mean?" Jake inquired, furrowing his brow.

"In this trial, you will navigate a labyrinth formed from the whispers of the woods," Seraphina explained. "The echoes will call to you, trying to lead you astray. You must listen closely and discern the truth from the distractions. Only by working together and trusting one another can you find your way."

"Sounds like it could get tricky," Mandy said, feeling a mix of excitement and apprehension. "But we can do it if we stick together."

As they approached the entrance to the labyrinth, the trees parted to reveal a winding path lined with tall hedges that seemed to pulse with energy. The whispers grew louder, swirling around them like a tempest.

"Stay focused," Don reminded them, taking a deep breath as they stepped into the labyrinth. "Let's keep our eyes and ears open."

The moment they entered, the air shifted, and the whispers became a cacophony of sounds. Voices echoed around them, mingling with the rustling leaves.

"Turn back! You don't belong here!" one voice warned, while another sweetly coaxed, "Follow me! I will show you the way."

"What do we do?" Jake asked, feeling overwhelmed by the conflicting sounds.

"Listen to each other," Mandy replied, her heart racing. "We need to focus on our bond and trust that we can guide each other."

As they ventured deeper into the labyrinth, the whispers intensified, becoming more chaotic. "This way!" one voice urged. "No, over here!" another insisted.

"Don't listen to them!" Timmy shouted, trying to block out the distractions. "We need to stay true to our instincts!"

"Stick together!" Don called, leading the way as they navigated the winding paths. "We can't let the echoes confuse us!"

They continued forward, but the whispers grew louder, swirling around them like a storm. Suddenly, the path forked into two, and each path seemed equally inviting.

"I think we should go left," Jake suggested, glancing down the dimly lit corridor.

"No, I feel like right is the way to go!" Mandy countered, uncertainty flickering in her eyes. "I can hear something."

"Maybe we should split up," Timmy proposed, feeling the pressure mounting. "We can cover more ground."

"No!" Don exclaimed, shaking his head firmly. "We need to stay together. The echoes are trying to separate us. We must choose one path and trust that we're making the right decision together."

The friends exchanged determined looks, their bond strengthening as they stood united against the chaos of the whispers. "Let's go left," Timmy finally said, his voice steady. "We'll go with our instincts."

With that decision made, they turned left and pressed on, the whispers growing quieter as they moved deeper into the labyrinth. Each step felt heavy with anticipation, and they could feel the weight of the trial bearing down upon them.

After what felt like an eternity, they reached a clearing surrounded by towering hedges. In the center stood a large, shimmering mirror, its surface reflecting their anxious faces.

"Is this part of the trial?" Jake asked, eyeing the mirror warily.

"The Mirror of Echoes," Seraphina explained, appearing beside them once more. "It reflects not only your appearance but also your fears and doubts. To move forward, you must confront what you see."

The friends hesitated, exchanging uncertain glances. "What if it shows us something terrible?" Mandy whispered, her heart pounding.

"Whatever it reveals, we will face it together," Don assured them, his voice steady. "We've come this far. We can't turn back now."

One by one, they approached the mirror, their hearts racing. As they gazed into its depths, the reflections began to shift and change.

Don stepped up first, peering into the mirror. His reflection warped, revealing a version of himself shrouded in darkness, filled with fear and uncertainty. "You're not strong enough," the reflection taunted. "You'll fail when it counts."

"Get out of my head!" Don shouted, clenching his fists. "I am strong! I've faced darkness before!"

The reflection flickered and began to dissolve, but a wave of fear washed over him, lingering at the edges of his mind. He took a deep breath, grounding himself. "I have my friends with me. I won't let fear control me."

With a surge of determination, Don stepped back, allowing the next friend to face the mirror.

Mandy approached, her heart racing as she gazed into the shimmering surface. She saw a reflection of herself surrounded by shadows, each one whispering doubts. "You're not worthy," they hissed. "You'll let everyone down."

"No!" Mandy exclaimed, shaking her head. "I have proven my worth through every challenge we faced together!"

As she spoke, the shadows began to recede, and the reflection brightened, showing her standing strong alongside her friends. She smiled, feeling the light within her flourish.

Timmy stepped forward next, the weight of anticipation heavy on his shoulders. As he looked into the mirror, he saw himself struggling against the waves of the ocean, fear coursing through him. "You'll drown," the reflection taunted. "You can't handle the depths!"

"No!" Timmy shouted, his voice echoing through the clearing. "I've learned to embrace my magic! I am strong enough to overcome any challenge!"

With that proclamation, the reflection wavered, and the water transformed into a gentle stream. Timmy stepped back, a smile breaking across his face.

Finally, it was Jake's turn. He approached the mirror, his heart pounding in his chest. The reflection shifted, revealing shadows creeping in around him, whispering dark thoughts. "You're alone," it hissed. "No one will stand by you."

But Jake took a deep breath, recalling the bond they had forged. "I am not alone!" he declared, his voice ringing clear. "I have my friends, and together, we are stronger than any shadow!"

With that, the shadows dissipated, and his reflection brightened, showing him standing proudly with his friends.

As the last of the reflections faded, the friends gathered together, feeling the weight of the trial lift from their shoulders

They turned away from the mirror, the whispers of the woods growing louder, guiding them toward the next part of their journey. They followed the path, a sense of unity driving them forward.

Chapter 24: The Heart of the Woods

With the echoes of their fears behind them, Don, Mandy, Timmy, and Jake ventured deeper into the Whispering Woods. The atmosphere was thick with anticipation, the whispers swirling around them like a gentle breeze urging them onward. They had faced their doubts, emerged victorious, and now the path ahead beckoned them toward greater challenges.

"Can you feel that?" Mandy asked, glancing at the trees around them. "It's like the woods are alive, watching us."

"I can," Timmy replied, his eyes scanning the branches above. "It's as if they're guiding us toward something important."

As they continued walking, the path began to narrow, winding through tall, ancient trees with twisted roots and gnarled branches. The sunlight filtered through the leaves, casting intricate patterns on the ground. The further they ventured, the more the atmosphere changed, becoming charged with magic.

"I wonder what the next trial will be," Don mused, a mix of excitement and apprehension coursing through him. "We've faced shadows and echoes. What else could the woods throw at us?"

"I think we should be prepared for anything," Jake said, his expression serious. "But we've come so far already. We can handle whatever comes next."

Suddenly, the whispers grew louder, intertwining with the sounds of rustling leaves. The friends halted, exchanging glances filled with both excitement and trepidation. "It's like they're speaking to us," Mandy said, straining to listen.

"Can you understand what they're saying?" Timmy asked, tilting his head.

"It's more like a feeling," she replied. "I sense something significant lies ahead, but it feels... bittersweet."

Just then, a shimmering figure emerged from the trees—a tall, graceful woman with flowing hair that seemed to ripple like water. Her eyes sparkled with the colors of the forest, and her presence radiated warmth and wisdom.

"Welcome, guardians," she said, her voice soft yet powerful. "I am Elysia, the Spirit of the Woods. You have come far on your journey, but the next trial will test your bonds and your understanding of sacrifice."

"Sacrifice?" Don echoed, feeling a chill run down his spine. "What does that mean?"

"The Heart of the Woods is a sacred place where magic flows strongest," Elysia explained, her gaze piercing yet kind. "But it is also a place of choice. You must each make a sacrifice to prove your dedication to protecting the magic of the sanctuary."

Mandy stepped forward, her heart pounding. "What kind of sacrifices are we talking about?"

"Each guardian will face a choice that reflects their deepest desires and fears," Elysia said. "To move forward, you must let go of something you hold dear."

The friends exchanged worried glances, the weight of Elysia's words sinking in. "I don't want to lose anything," Timmy said, a hint of fear in his voice. "What if it's something I can't get back?"

"Trust in the magic of the woods," Elysia reassured them. "What you sacrifice may lead to greater understanding and strength. Remember that your bonds with one another are what truly matter."

"Okay," Don said, stepping forward. "We can do this together. We've faced darkness, and we've faced our fears. We can face this trial, too."

As Elysia gestured for them to follow, the friends moved deeper into the woods, the air thickening with anticipation. The trees parted to reveal a stunning clearing filled with vibrant flowers and luminous plants, their colors pulsating with energy.

In the center of the clearing stood a massive tree, its trunk wider than any they had seen before. The leaves glowed softly, casting a gentle light over the area. "This is the Heart of the Woods," Elysia announced, her voice echoing through the clearing.

As they approached the tree, they could feel a powerful magic emanating from it. "To begin the trial, each of you must place your hand upon the tree and face your choice," Elysia instructed. "Trust in yourselves, and the magic will guide you."

Don nodded, feeling a mix of determination and apprehension. He stepped forward, placing his hand on the warm bark of the tree. The moment he made contact, a wave of energy surged through him, and visions flooded his mind.

He saw himself standing in the sanctuary, filled with joy and laughter, surrounded by his friends. But then, the images shifted. He saw a vision of darkness creeping back into the sanctuary, threatening everything he held dear.

"No!" he shouted, feeling a surge of panic. The vision shifted again, showing him standing alone, the shadows closing in. "I can't lose my friends!" he cried, his heart racing.

Suddenly, the vision transformed again, revealing a choice. He saw two paths before him—one leading to power and glory, the other leading to sacrifice and unity. The choice felt heavy, and he could feel the weight of each option pressing down on him.

"I choose to protect my friends," he declared, the words echoing in the clearing. "I will sacrifice my desire for power to ensure our bonds remain strong!"

As he spoke, the energy surged through him, illuminating the clearing with a bright light. The tree responded, glowing even brighter as if acknowledging his choice.

Feeling a sense of relief, Don stepped back, watching as his friends approached the tree one by one.

Mandy placed her hand on the trunk, feeling the warmth radiate from it. Instantly, visions flooded her mind. She saw herself in the sanctuary, surrounded by flowers and magic. But then the vision darkened, revealing a future filled with loneliness and doubt.

"No!" she gasped, pulling back slightly. "I won't allow myself to be consumed by fear!"

The vision shifted again, showing her a path filled with connections and love, but it required her to let go of something she cherished. "I will sacrifice my fear of failure," she said, her voice steady. "I choose to trust in the magic of our friendship!"

As she spoke, a wave of energy washed over her, the tree responding to her declaration. Light enveloped her, filling the clearing with warmth and reassurance.

Next, it was Timmy's turn. He approached the tree, placing his hand on its trunk. As he did, visions flooded his mind—memories of the ocean and the power of the tides. But soon, those memories twisted into darkness, revealing a future filled with chaos and despair.

"No!" he shouted, feeling the weight of the shadows pressing in on him. "I won't let fear control my destiny!"

The vision shifted again, revealing a choice between power and vulnerability. "I will sacrifice my need for control," he proclaimed. "I choose to embrace the flow of life and trust my friends!"

With that declaration, the energy surged, illuminating the clearing once more. The tree glowed brighter, the magic responding to Timmy's choice.

Finally, it was Jake's turn. He stepped forward, heart racing as he placed his hand on the tree. Instantly, he was flooded with visions—images of strength and bravery but also of loneliness and doubt.

"Will I ever be enough?" the echo of his own voice whispered. Shadows crept in, whispering doubts that threatened to consume him.

"No!" Jake shouted, shaking his head. "I refuse to let fear dictate my path!"

The visions transformed, revealing two paths before him—one filled with glory and isolation, the other filled with connection and sacrifice. "I choose to sacrifice my desire for recognition!" he declared, his voice ringing clear. "I choose friendship over glory!"

As he spoke, the magic surged through him, illuminating the clearing one last time. The tree responded, its energy wrapping around the friends, binding them together in a radiant display of light.

The clearing filled with warmth as they stood united, their hearts intertwined. The whispers of the woods swirled around them, a melody of joy and harmony.

Elysia appeared, her expression proud. "You have faced the Trial of Echoes and made choices that reflect your true selves. Each sacrifice you made has strengthened your bond as guardians."

The friends exchanged proud smiles, feeling the weight of the trial lift from their shoulders. They had faced their fears and emerged stronger, united by the choices they had made.

Chapter 25: Secrets of the Woods

The atmosphere in the Whispering Woods shimmered with newfound energy as Don, Mandy, Timmy, and Jake emerged from the clearing where they had faced the Trial of Echoes. Their hearts were light, buoyed by the choices they had made and the strength of their bond. Yet, as they continued deeper into the woods, they sensed that more revelations awaited them.

"I can't believe we did it!" Mandy exclaimed, her eyes sparkling with excitement. "Facing our fears was intense, but we proved that we're stronger together!"

"Yeah, it felt great to let go of what was holding us back," Timmy added, a sense of relief washing over him. "I feel like we're more connected than ever."

Jake nodded, his face serious but hopeful. "But we have to stay focused. Elysia mentioned that there are more secrets to uncover in the woods. I think we're only beginning to understand the true magic here."

As they ventured forward, the air grew thick with anticipation. The trees began to sway gently, as if whispering secrets to one another. Sunlight filtered through the branches, illuminating the path ahead in a warm golden glow.

"Do you think we'll find more trials?" Don asked, glancing at his friends. "Or perhaps something unexpected?"

"Let's just stay open to whatever comes our way," Mandy suggested. "We've proven we can handle surprises."

Suddenly, the path opened into another clearing, revealing a breathtaking sight. In the center stood a magnificent fountain, its waters cascading gracefully over intricate stone carvings of magical creatures. The air was filled with the soothing sound of water flowing, and colorful flowers adorned the edges of the fountain, their petals glimmering in the sunlight.

"Wow," Jake breathed, stepping closer. "This is incredible!"

As they approached, they noticed that the water sparkled with an ethereal light, reflecting hues of blue and green. "It looks like the water is enchanted," Timmy observed, kneeling down to touch the surface. As he did, ripples danced across the water, and a soft voice emerged from within.

"Welcome, brave guardians," the voice echoed gently. "I am Aquara, the spirit of the fountain. You have proven your courage, but the woods hold more secrets. To unlock them, you must answer my riddle."

"A riddle?" Don asked, excitement bubbling within him. "We're ready!"

Aquara smiled, the water shimmering with energy. "Listen closely. Here is your riddle: I am not alive, but I can grow; I do not have lungs, but I need air. What am I?"

The friends exchanged glances, their minds racing as they contemplated the riddle. "This is a good one!" Jake said, furrowing his brow in thought.

"Hmm..." Timmy began, biting his lip. "It's something that can grow without being alive. What could it be?"

"I'm thinking," Mandy said slowly, "what needs air but isn't alive? What about... fire?"

"Fire!" Don exclaimed, his eyes lighting up. "It needs air to burn, but it's not alive. That has to be it!"

"Fire!" the friends echoed together, a sense of triumph swelling within them.

Aquara's laughter rang through the air, a melodic sound that echoed softly. "You are correct! Fire is indeed the answer."

As the words left their lips, the water in the fountain glowed brightly, and a stream of light shot forth, enveloping the friends. "You have proven your wisdom," Aquara continued, "and for that, I will share a secret of the woods."

The water shimmered, and images began to form within the fountain—visions of the Whispering Woods in their past glory, vibrant and filled with life. They saw spirits dancing, laughter echoing through the trees, and creatures of all shapes and sizes celebrating the magic around them.

"But then…" Timmy said, his voice trailing off as the visions shifted. They saw darkness creeping into the woods, consuming the joy and magic. "What happened?"

"The darkness has always sought to corrupt the magic of the woods," Aquara explained, her tone somber. "It preys on fear and doubt, seeking to disrupt the harmony we have built. But there is hope. You, as guardians, hold the power to protect this magic."

"What can we do?" Mandy asked, her determination renewed. "How can we help?"

"To maintain the balance," Aquara replied, "you must journey to the Grove of Whispers, where the ancient spirits reside. There, you will find the Heartstone, a powerful artifact that binds the magic of the woods. It is essential for keeping the darkness at bay."

"The Heartstone?" Jake echoed, intrigued. "Where is this Grove of Whispers?"

"Follow the sound of the whispering winds," Aquara instructed, her voice a gentle breeze. "They will guide you to the grove. But beware—dark forces may attempt to hinder your progress. Trust in one another and listen to the magic of the woods."

With a newfound sense of purpose, the friends thanked Aquara for her guidance and set off in the direction of the whispers. The path wound through the trees, the air thick with anticipation as they moved deeper into the woods.

As they walked, the whispers became a symphony of sounds, guiding them forward. The trees swayed gently, their leaves rustling as if encouraging them along the way. The atmosphere felt alive, charged with energy as they followed the beckoning calls of the woods.

After a while, they reached a fork in the path. "Which way do we go?" Timmy asked, glancing between the two trails.

"I think we should listen to the whispers," Mandy suggested, closing her eyes to focus. "It feels like they're urging us to the right."

"Let's go right, then!" Don agreed, feeling the magic guiding them.

The friends took the right path, feeling the energy of the woods swirl around them. The trees closed in, creating a canopy of vibrant greens and browns. As they ventured further, the whispers grew louder, guiding them toward their destination.

Suddenly, the air shifted, and they heard a low growl echoing through the trees. "What was that?" Jake asked, his heart racing.

"Stay alert!" Don warned, glancing around cautiously. "We might not be alone."

As they continued down the path, the shadows around them thickened, and the whispers turned to frantic murmurs. "They're coming!" a voice warned, trembling with fear. "Run!"

Before they could react, dark figures emerged from the shadows—twisted creatures that lurked at the edges of the woods. Their eyes glowed with malice, and their forms shifted in and out of view, like living shadows.

"Defend yourselves!" Timmy shouted, raising his hands in preparation.

The friends instinctively gathered together, their magical items glowing brightly as they stood united against the encroaching darkness. "We've faced shadows before!" Don declared, his voice steady. "We can do this!"

As the dark creatures lunged forward, the friends unleashed their combined magic. "Feel the light!" Mandy shouted, channeling her energy into the air.

The magic surged forth, illuminating the clearing in a brilliant flash. The dark creatures recoiled, hissing in fury as they were pushed back by the radiant energy.

"Keep pushing!" Jake urged, feeling the strength of their unity. "We can drive them away!"

With each wave of light, the shadows grew weaker, and the creatures faltered. The friends worked in harmony, focusing their energy and trust in one another.

As the last of the darkness retreated, the whispers returned, echoing through the woods, urging them onward. "You are strong!" they called. "You have faced the shadows!"

Breathing heavily, the friends regrouped, their hearts racing. "That was intense!" Timmy exclaimed, feeling the adrenaline coursing through him. "We handled it well."

"Together," Don said, nodding with determination. "We can face anything."

As they continued on their path, they could feel the energy of the woods shifting again. "We must be close to the Grove of Whispers," Mandy said, glancing around.

Suddenly, they reached a clearing bathed in soft, ethereal light. Before them lay the Grove of Whispers, an enchanting space filled with glowing trees and shimmering flowers. At the center stood a large stone pedestal, atop which rested a magnificent Heartstone, pulsing with radiant energy.

"The Heartstone!" Jake exclaimed, his eyes wide with wonder. "We found it!"

As they stepped closer, the whispers grew louder, surrounding them with a symphony of voices. "Guardians of the magic, you have come to reclaim the Heartstone. Your journey has prepared you for this moment."

Eagerly, they approached the pedestal, feeling the warmth radiating from the Heartstone. "What do we do?" Timmy asked, glancing at the others.

"Trust in the magic of the woods," Seraphina advised, appearing beside them. "Only by uniting your powers will you be able to claim the Heartstone."

The friends gathered around the pedestal, their hands hovering above the Heartstone. They could feel its energy pulsing beneath their fingers, beckoning them closer.

"On three," Don said, determination filling his voice. "One... two... three!"

They placed their hands on the Heartstone simultaneously, and an explosion of light engulfed them. The energy surged through their bodies, connecting them in a web of magic and unity.

As the light intensified, they felt the weight of the woods' history and magic flow through them. Visions flooded their minds—images of guardians who had come before them, their struggles and triumphs intertwining with their own journey.

In that moment, they understood the true power of their bond and the responsibility they carried as guardians. The Heartstone pulsed with life, responding to their connection.

With a final surge of energy, the light enveloped them, illuminating the Grove of Whispers with brilliance. The whispers of the woods sang a triumphant melody, celebrating their unity and courage.

As the light faded, they stood together, the Heartstone now glowing brightly atop the pedestal. They had proven themselves worthy, and the magic of the woods flowed through them.